SECRET MISSION #1:
THE DOOM BOX

BY GREG FARSHTEY

SCHOLASTIC INC.

No part of this publication may be reproduced, stored in a retrieval system, or transmitted in any form or by any means, electronic, mechanical, photocopying, recording, or otherwise, without written permission of the publisher. For information regarding permission, write to Scholastic Inc., Attention: Permissions Department, 557 Broadway, New York, NY 10012.

ISBN 978-0-545-46516-8

LEGO, the LEGO logo, the Brick and Knob configurations are trademarks of the LEGO Group. © 2012 The LEGO Group. Produced by Scholastic Inc. under license from the LEGO Group.

Published by Scholastic Inc. SCHOLASTIC and associated logos are trademarks and/or registered trademarks of Scholastic Inc.

12 11 10 9 8 7 6 5 4 3 2 1   12 13 14 15 16 17/0

Printed in the U.S.A.   40

First printing, September 2012

Prologue

5,000 Years Ago

The four hooded figures cautiously approached the well of flame. The fire cast bizarre shadows on the stone walls of the chamber and filled the air with smoke that burned the eyes. As they drew closer, the beings felt the intense heat. Like a physical blow, it forced them back a step before sheer determination kept them moving forward.

When they were within three steps of the well, each of the beings produced a set of long metal tongs. With perfectly coordinated movements, they extended the tongs into the flames. A moment later, they lifted a small box from the fire.

It did not look at all impressive. The box was perhaps one foot by two feet square, and made of simple, unadorned black metal. It had no obvious lid or handle or any other way to open it. There was no lock of any kind. It appeared to be simply a block of iron, glowing red-hot.

Carefully, they set the box down on a stone pedestal. All four pairs of tongs were then set aside. Two of the figures stepped back into the shadows. A third knelt down in front of the box, examining it closely, while the fourth peered over his shoulder.

"Is it complete?" asked Deneb, the watcher.

Arctur, the examiner, nodded once.

"Will it . . . ?" Deneb said, his voice trailing off.

"Work?" said Arctur. "Yes, may the fates forgive us, I believe it will."

Deneb gave an anxious smile. "Imagine—the means to eliminate anyone or anything we choose. All we have to do is activate the box and . . ."

Arctur stood, his eyes never leaving the box. "No."

Deneb's eyebrows rose. "What are you saying?"

Arctur turned and walked away from the box. Deneb took a step forward and bent low as if to pick it up. At a signal from Arctur, the other two figures took hold of Deneb and gently pulled him away from their creation.

"No," said Arctur. "We will not be using it."

"What?" Deneb shouted. "After all we have done, all we have sacrificed, the actions we have taken that can never be undone? We have made ourselves outcasts from the civilized galaxy, monsters in the eyes of the natives of a thousand worlds, all to create this box—and you say we won't be using it?"

"That is what I said," said Arctur. "It will never be used. It will be destroyed immediately."

"But why? I demand to know!"

Arctur wheeled on Deneb, his hood flying off to reveal ancient reptilian features. "Because, you fool, it cannot be turned off!"

An uneasy silence settled on the chamber. All four beings knew exactly what Arctur's words meant. Left unchecked, the box was not just a tool for espionage or even a weapon of war. It was certain doom for every living thing in the galaxy, and perhaps beyond.

In three quick strides, Arctur crossed the chamber and snatched up a glowing axe. Energy streamed from the blade as he brought it down upon the box. There was a blinding flash upon impact, as the energies of the weapon met those of the box. When those present could see again, the sight of the box split into three pieces awaited them. The air sizzled with raw power unleashed.

Arctur looked at the axe, now just a piece of metal, its energy spent. "This will have to do, then. We will take the three pieces and scatter them in the farthest reaches of the galaxy, where no one will ever find them. Only then will the known worlds be safe from our creation."

Solemnly, he began telling the others of the planets where the pieces should be taken. All listened carefully . . . so much so that no one noticed Deneb as he stood in the shadows, carving something into the stone wall.

It was only a thousand years ago that the chamber was rediscovered. The treasure hunters who stumbled upon it did not find the jewels and precious metals they sought. Instead, all they saw was the site of a long-burnt-out fire and what looked like the crude scrawls of a child on one of the walls. It was a crushing disappointment.

At least, it was, until one of the explorers noticed that the carvings on the wall weren't just random scratches. They made up a map of the galaxy, with three particular planets marked with the symbol of a square. Unsure of just what it all meant, the looters used lasers to cut the map out of the wall and hauled it away.

This turned out to be a bad idea. Robed beings started popping up wherever the treasure hunters went, trying to get the map back. There were fights on many worlds, most of which the thieves lost. In desperation, they made a deal with a crooked trader, swapping the map for a fast ship . . . and disappearing from our story.

The trader was smart enough to know he had something potentially valuable, but also something that might attract the wrong kind of attention. At best, Hero Factory might show up and arrest him for possession of a stolen artifact. At worst, those robed guys would appear, take it away from him, and wreck his whole business in the process. The best thing to do, he decided, was to sell it—fast.

So that's what he did. He got lucky enough to meet up with a criminal looking to spend his loot, and he made a deal for the map. What happened to it after that was a mystery, not the least to the robed pursuers of the tablet, who never found a trace of it again.

As it turned out, two Hero Factory Heroes, Stormer and Bulk, came close to finding it not long after. But the leader of Alpha Team and his powerful teammate didn't know anything about it at the time, or its potential value, so they weren't looking for it.

What things? Well, the galaxy might not be a few hours away from complete destruction, for one. But maybe we had better begin a little closer to the beginning. . . .

1

Stormer walked quickly down the hallway of Hero Factory Headquarters, Subbasement 2. The only sound was his metal feet clanging against the floor. Of course, there could have been a herd of angry mudstompers running toward him and he wouldn't have noticed — not with the crisis he faced today.

Like the other Heroes of Hero Factory, Stormer was a robot. Also like the others, he didn't like that word much. It seemed too simple and crude. Each Hero had unique powers and personalities, and was able to fight evil on their own or as part of a team. Some were strong, some were quick, some were skilled planners, and others had wild imaginations — they were much more than walking machines powered by the Hero Cores in their chests.

Today, Stormer almost wished he was some big, lumbering metal thing that just did what it was programmed to do. Then he wouldn't have to think, or worry, or imagine what was going to happen if his team failed in their next mission. But he was a Hero Factory veteran and Alpha Team leader, and worrying came with the job.

Stormer glanced at the multiscreen computer console on the wall. Displayed were the names and ugly faces of criminals recently captured by his team after their shocking breakout from Hero Factory, including such major threats as Splitface, Toxic Reapa, and Jawblade. A touch of a button brought up the faces of those still at large: Core Hunter, XT4, Thornraxx, Speeda Demon, and Voltix.

Hero Factory had never experienced a major breakout prior to this year. When it came, it was every bit the disaster one would expect.

Dozens of criminals were unleashed on the galaxy and it was a full-time job to catch and cuff them. It was a much bigger task than local planetary police forces could handle, but exactly the kind of mission Hero Factory was made for.

For the moment, Speeda Demon had disappeared, but Stormer was confident he would turn up again soon. He stole for the thrill of it, so no amount of loot would ever satisfy him. They would get him eventually.

As for Core Hunter, that was more troubling. His last crimes prior to his imprisonment at Hero Factory had been strange, even for him. Since his escape, reports indicated he might have been planning a return to the scenes of his last thefts. Why, Stormer wondered—was he planning to rob those places again?

Stormer did not turn at the sound of Zib entering the room. Zib was one of the most experienced Mission Managers in Hero Factory and was often the only lifeline for a team out in the field. He had more information packed in his head than the average computer, not to mention the skill to patch up a damaged robot in an emergency.

"We need to talk," said Zib. "I have a message from Mr. Makuro."

Stormer wasn't surprised. The breakout had been a humiliation for Makuro, the founder of Hero Factory, and he wanted constant updates on the recapture effort.

"Tell him there's nothing new to tell him," said Stormer. "The team is back for a little rest and training. We leave again in thirty hours."

The small, silver robot shook his head. "You will be leaving before sunrise. You have a new mission."

Stormer wheeled on Zib. "What new mission? The breakout was designated Priority 1-A, on Mr. Makuro's orders!"

"This mission is Priority 1-A Delta Red, Stormer," Zib answered quietly.

The leader of Alpha Team stared at the Mission Manager in silence. The Delta Red designation was used only when the galaxy itself was in danger of destruction. Even a massive asteroid headed right for Hero Factory wouldn't trigger a D-R code. A second breakout could have happened right then and the Heroes would have had to ignore it in favor of the Delta Red mission.

"Explain," said Stormer.

Zib handed over a small disk. "What we know is on the disk. View it immediately and then brief your team for action."

Zib turned to go, but Stormer's voice stopped him. "Zib, Alpha Team is exhausted. They've captured a dozen criminals in the last four weeks without time for refit and repair. I can take over leadership of another squad and—"

"Another squad won't be Alpha Team," Zib replied, his back to Stormer. "You and yours are the best, and only the best will be good enough this time."

Even as these words were spoken, some of the "best" were having their problems. Bulk, Furno, and Surge had activated a training room program, then gotten into an argument over which one had captured more escaped villains. One thing led to another, and eventually the danger level of the room got turned up past maximum. The controls had promptly shorted out and the "obstacles" in the room had run wild.

"Um, whose idea was this again?" asked Bulk. He was suspended from the ceiling by poly-duranium wire, one of the strongest substances in the universe, and he wasn't happy about it.

"You should talk," said Furno, wiping fire-retardant foam off his armor. As soon as he made the move to do so, jets sprouted out of the walls and sprayed more all over him, leaving him looking like a very large ice cream sundae.

Surge didn't say anything. He had been trapped in a zero-gravity zone for the last fifteen minutes and it was starting to make even a robot a little queasy. All he could do was turn end over end, occasionally smacking into Bulk.

"How do we shut this crazy room down?" asked Bulk, trying and failing to shift into a more comfortable position.

"Hit the 'off' switch?" suggested Furno.

"We broke it, remember? It's on fire."

"Okay, it's a timed program, so we wait for the time to run out."

Bulk shook his head. "We broke the timer too."

Furno sighed. "Then I think that leaves waiting for somebody to come looking for us. With our luck, it will be Stormer."

"Hey," said Bulk. "Maybe I got an idea."

"Maybe?"

"Well, I wouldn't bet my Hero Core on it, but it might work," said Bulk. "We'll only get one try, though. You gotta move fast, Furno, and duck faster."

"I can do that," said Furno.

"Okay, move three steps to your right and then head for the 'off' switch. When I say drop, drop. Got it?"

Furno did a quick sidestep, then raced forward. He had only gone a few steps when he heard Bulk shout, "Down!" The rookie Hero hit the floor as a jet of foam sailed over his head and struck the burning switch, putting out the fire.

"Great!" Furno said, getting to his feet and being soaked with more foam in the process. "Now we can turn this dumb room off."

"Not so fast, kid," said Bulk. "You're gonna need to give that switch a good whack to make it work now, and I'm not up to the job—or rather, I'm too far up for the job. Plus you know there are sixty-seven booby traps between you and it."

"Breez says sixty-six," Furno pointed out.

Bulk smiled. "Breez doesn't know about the supersecret one. Anyway, what we need to do is hit it hard and fast with some kind of a missile."

Furno looked around. "I don't see anything we can use."

"I do," Bulk said, with a chuckle. "I think I can get one foot free, and—"

Surge had drifted near again. Bulk lashed out with a kick and sent his partner flying across the room to crash into the off switch. Instantly, the wires retracted and Bulk fell to the floor with a thud.

Furno rushed over to check on him and Surge, grateful that the foam jets had shut down as well. Bulk was fine, but Surge was looking to change that.

"You big, overstuffed—" The blue Hero snarled, stalking toward Bulk. "What did you think you were doing, kicking me like that?"

Bulk shrugged. "Saving our pride, pal," he answered. "But if you have a beef, let's hear it."

Electricity crackled from Surge's armored fingers. "How do you like your beef cooked, Bulk?"

Stormer's voice cut through the room. "Stand down, Surge, right now."

The Alpha Team leader stood in the doorway, eyeing the disaster area the room had become. Bulk took a step toward him, saying, "My fault. Things got a little out of hand."

"I'll worry about putting you three on disciplinary duty next week, if we're all still alive," Stormer answered. "Zib needs us in the briefing room. Furno, scrape that gunk off your armor on the way. You're Heroes—try acting like it."

Evo, Rocka, and Breez were already assembled around the briefing table when Stormer and the others arrived. On the screen were images of three objects. They were all roughly the same shape, with jagged edges, and looked like the shattered pieces of something a few feet square. But even with the naked eye, it was obvious that these three puzzle pieces could never fit together. The sides simply didn't match in any way, so there was no clear path to joining them with one another.

"What's that?" asked Furno. "Looks like . . . junk."

"And it may well be," answered Zib. "But someone thinks it is valuable junk."

"Run it down for them," said Stormer. "We may not have much time."

"Yes, yes, of course," said Zib. "Here are the facts as we know them: Seven years ago, these items were among the loot stolen in three separate robberies committed by Core Hunter. Strangely enough, in each case, he ignored potentially valuable items in favor of these fragments. Hero Factory's help was requested and he was eventually arrested and jailed. That is where he remained until the recent breakout."

"What about the stuff?" asked Furno. "Did we get it back?"

"Negative," said Zib. "None of the three items were recovered at the time, nor have they surfaced since."

"So what do you think?" asked Breez. "Abandoned? Destroyed?"

Stormer shook his head. "Hidden. Best guess is he stashed the items before capture. Now that he's on the loose again, we think he's trying to reclaim them . . . and that's what we have to stop."

Stormer hit a button. The screen changed to a galaxy map with three distant points flashing. "Our mission is to recapture Core Hunter and recover those fragments. If we can do only one . . . getting those objects is the priority."

"What?!" Furno exclaimed. "We're going to let a dangerous criminal run wild so we can collect the trash?"

Stormer's eyes bored into Furno. "At ease, Hero. I said *if* we can do only one — I expect us to do both, and will accept nothing less. Clear?"

Furno started to say something, then evidently thought better of it and just nodded his agreement. It was pretty obviously not the day to argue with Stormer.

Stormer turned back to the group. "I've asked Zib to load the Hero Logs of those three crimes. We are going to review them and look for clues as to where Core Hunter hid the objects."

Bulk leaned forward and put his hands on the conference table. He had known Stormer a long time, and had seen the Alpha Team leader in every mood from happy to guilty to furious. This was the first time he had ever detected a note of fear in Stormer's voice. "How bad is it?" he asked.

"Bad as can be," Stormer replied. "If we foul this one up, there won't be a Hero Factory to come back to . . . or anything else. So face front, Heroes, and pay attention — missions don't come any bigger than this."

2

tormer and his team sat in the briefing room, watching as the large screen flared to life. An instant later, they heard the recorded voice of Bulk. . . .

Mission Log, Bulk recording—I have been dispatched to a planet in the Omega system to investigate reports of a break-in and robbery at a government vault. It sounds like something the locals should be able to handle, but they asked for a Hero, and they got one.

For the second time, Bulk reviewed what was known about this planet. It was essentially a big bank. Residents of planets all over the quadrant left their valuables here.

Bulk stepped out of his Hero craft. A trio of local officials, short, blue, humanoid-looking robots, was waiting to greet him. Antennae were mounted on their heads and intermittently flashed bright light. At first, Bulk thought they were angry at him, since they weren't saying anything. Then he gave his translator a whack and its mechanical voice began to speak. On this world, all communication was done through the flashing of the antennae lights, instead of speech.

"We Who Serve greet you, Hero," said the three, bowing toward Bulk. He gave a quick bow back.

"Yeah, nice to be here," said Bulk. "Can you guys understand me okay?"

The three nodded. "We can translate the electrical impulses that become your words."

Bulk chuckled. "So in other words, you know what I'm going to say before I do."

The three robots obviously didn't get the joke, but smiled slightly anyway. Then they turned and beckoned for Bulk to follow. They walked quickly through streets teeming with traffic, mostly more blue robots flying with personal rocket packs. Bulk had to keep ducking to avoid getting hit. The relatively small size of most of the inhabitants meant low-flying was generally permitted.

The building housing the vault was an imposing-looking pile of stone, with no visible entrance. Bulk was just about to ask how they were supposed to get inside when the three robots passed their right hands over a bare patch of ground. The earth opened up, revealing a staircase leading underground.

"There is nothing actually in the building," said We Who Serve. "It is only there for the sake of visitors. They expect to see such a thing. We keep all our secure items beneath the soil."

Bulk followed them down several flights of stairs. The air went from cool to cold as they descended. Bulk did a quick scan of the security systems in place along the way. They were impressive, to say the least. Ultrasensitive alarms, bars made of some of the toughest metals in the universe, anti-tampering devices on every lock—if a security system existed and could stop a theft, it was here. How, then, he wondered, had anyone managed to steal anything?

After traversing for what felt like an hour through winding metal corridors, they came to a large vault—or, rather, what remained of a large vault. The door had been sliced open in such a way that nothing was left but the frame. The interior of the vault still held some items, including a bag of jewels and a broken crate.

Bulk took a closer look at the vault door. The edges of the frame were charred. "So someone blasted their way in, *after* managing to evade all the security in the building?" Bulk asked.

"No, no, no," said We Who Serve. "No one broke *into* the vault—someone or something broke *out*."

It took a second for that piece of news to sink in. Then Bulk found he couldn't help but smile. Whoever had planned this had some brains.

"Let me guess," he said. "All the security in this place is designed to keep people from getting in, not getting out. So all the thief had to do was sneak inside some other way and then it'd be easy to get out again with the loot."

The three blue robots looked down at the ground, as if a little ashamed that all their precautions had been defeated so easily. "We have the inventory of what was in that vault for you to review."

One of them handed over a pocket scanner. Bulk gave it a quick read-through. The vault was said to hold a small amount of precious gems, a crate of valuable machine parts, and what appeared to be a broken piece of something or other. It was the crate that caught his eye.

"Valuable machine parts?" he said. "Try 'disassembled thief.' Somebody dismantles our crook, packs him in a crate, and gets him stored in your vault. When the time's right, he puts himself back together, steals what he wants from the vault, and breaks out—very neat. But why leave the jewels?"

The three robots began flashing lights among themselves. Bulk guessed they were discussing how to implement new security procedures to stop this from happening again. He took the time to examine the vault more carefully.

That was when he saw it—hidden way in the back of the vault, almost lost in the shadows. Bulk reached in and emerged with a spent Hero Core. One of these would keep a Hero Factory agent powered up and fighting for justice. Removed, it made the Hero into a well-armed paperweight.

There was only one criminal Bulk could think of who would leave a Hero Core behind as a calling card.

"I think I might know your thief," Bulk said.

"You must leave immediately," said We Who Serve. "You must track this criminal and return the item that was stored here. Our reputation depends upon it."

Bulk shrugged. "He's probably off-world by now, but maybe . . ."

"Maybe?"

"Maybe he expects us to think that," Bulk continued. "Yeah, sure . . . what was the key to this robbery? Patience. Sitting in a crate day after day until the time was right to strike. So maybe he's going to hide on this planet until the heat is off, then make it to safety someplace else."

Bulk frowned and started thinking out loud. "Let's see, he wouldn't hide outdoors—too much chance of being spotted. Same with any high-traffic building. He needs a large building where there are plenty of places to hide."

As one, the three blue robots turned to look at Bulk. They had an idea of what place might fit Bulk's description, and they didn't like it one bit.

Mission Log, Supplemental, Bulk recording. My little buddies could only think of one place big enough for the thief—Core Hunter—to be hiding in. It's the main power plant for the city, so huge that, even when fully staffed, there are plenty of places to get lost. 'Course, that almost makes it the perfect place for an ambush.

Bulk's metal feet clanged on the metal floors of the power station. So much, he decided, for being sneaky. With all that noise, Core Hunter could have heard him coming from a star system away.

Well, good, Bulk thought. *Let him get nervous in whatever rat hole he's hiding in. Bulk is coming for him.*

Just like every other Hero of Hero Factory, Bulk had a personal grudge against Core Hunter. Once, the criminal had been a member of Hero Factory, a force for good in the galaxy. Then he went bad. He started out small, stealing and smuggling, then he moved on to being a bounty hunter. His preferred targets: Heroes. He became known for stealing the Hero Cores from the Heroes he fought and defeated, keeping them as trophies. He even had a special weapon designed just for the purpose of swiping cores.

A Hero without his Hero Core was powerless. If he got revived fast enough, he would be all right. If not . . . well, no Hero liked to think about that. Anyway, as far as everyone at Hero Factory was concerned, Core Hunter was the worst kind of traitor.

So far, Bulk had been searching the plant for four hours. He was beginning to wonder if Core Hunter might have spotted his approach and slipped out an exit. It was also beginning to sink in that if Core Hunter really wanted to stay hidden in this place, he probably could.

"Come on, creep," muttered Bulk. "Show yourself."

Suddenly, something wrapped itself around Bulk, pinning his arms to his sides. It was a metallic net. When he tried to free himself, he felt a jolt of electricity and the net grew tighter.

"Will this do?" said Core Hunter, laughing. He stepped out of the shadows atop one of the two main dynamos. "Nice to see some things don't change. You're still big and dumb. You walked right into this trap with your optic sensors wide open."

Bulk struggled against his bonds, but each time, he got another debilitating surge of electricity and the net constricted that much more. He knew if he lost his balance and fell, he would be helpless to stop Core Hunter from taking his Hero Core.

"I didn't figure they would send you for this one, Bulk," said Core Hunter. "With a planet this important, I would have expected Stormer or Stringer . . . you know, one of the ones with a working brain."

Bulk knew what Core Hunter was trying to do. He wanted to get the Hero angry, make him keep fighting the net . . . if Bulk did that, he would be as dumb as Core Hunter thought he was. But the villain thought he knew just what his opponent was going to do, and that gave Bulk an edge.

There was only one way to shut down a power net: overload it and burn it out. That wasn't an easy thing to do when you didn't have use of your arms or hands. Then again, they were standing in a power plant.

Bulk glanced at the dynamo Core Hunter was standing on and smiled. Then he charged, heading right for the big power generator.

"What are you doing?" Core Hunter yelled. When he saw that Bulk wasn't slowing, he leapt off the dynamo. The next instant, Bulk slammed right into the machine.

There was a bright flash and an awesome jolt that sent Bulk flying backward, to bash into the far wall. For a few moments, he was paralyzed, his systems scrambling to compensate for the sudden energy surge. Then his Hero Core reset itself and Bulk abruptly sat up, now free of the blackened and dead power net.

He didn't see Core Hunter anywhere. Maybe he was lying somewhere dazed, or maybe he was planning another attack. Bulk got to his feet. Sparks were still arcing from the dynamo.

Probably just blacked out half the city, he thought.

Bulk thought he heard something. It was hard to be sure over the sizzle and pop of the mangled power generator, but it sounded like metal being cut open.

He suddenly remembered a story about Core Hunter. One time, a Hero had almost captured him by sabotaging his getaway vehicle. Core Hunter retaliated by not only wrecking his pursuer's Hero craft, but using a computer virus to disable every other mode of transport on the planet. "I always get payment in kind," the villain had said before escaping.

The other dynamo!

Bulk ran as fast as he could across the floor of the plant. Even as he did, he knew he was going too slow. As he neared the second dynamo, he could see Core Hunter tearing out wiring from its insides.

"No! You'll blow the whole thing!" shouted Bulk.

"I thought that was the idea," Core Hunter replied, turning away from the dynamo. He started to run for the exit, yelling over his shoulder, "Your choice, Bulk — save the plant's workers, or stop me."

To Bulk's credit, he never hesitated. He turned a sharp right and slammed the alarm button on the wall. As soon as the siren began to sound, he knew the robot workers in the plant would start evacuating.

Then he raced to the sabotaged dynamo. It quickly became obvious he could do nothing. He wasn't a tech whiz, but even if he had been, there was way too much damage to fix in time. Bulk ran for the exit Core Hunter had used.

Just as he made it outside, the dynamo blew. The reinforced outer wall of the power plant collapsed, huge lightning bolts shooting from the gaping holes in the structure. Bulk threw himself on the ground and hugged it tight while an energy storm raged above his head. It would be, he later said, the longest few minutes of his existence.

When it was over, Core Hunter was nowhere to be found. The three blue robots informed Bulk that a ship had been stolen and used to escape the surface of the planet. The thief had gotten away.

Still, there had been some small victory. Core Hunter wasn't carrying anything on him that looked like the object he'd stolen. He wouldn't have had time to retrieve it before stealing the ship, not unless he had added superspeed to his list of attributes. That meant it was on this planet . . . somewhere. But where?

Think he hid it in the power plant?" Furno asked when the recording was done.

"We searched through the rubble," Bulk answered. "Nothing."

"Destroyed in the blast?" asked Stringer.

"I don't think this thing is that easy to destroy," said Stormer. "I think Bulk was right the first time—he didn't have it with him when he went in there. He ditched it on the way, or passed it off to someone else."

"Zib, bring up a map of the area," said Nex. "Maybe we'll spot something."

The screen shifted to a satellite view of the power plant and its surroundings. The Heroes studied it for a moment before Stringer pointed to a spot just north of the power plant and said, "What about there?"

Stormer's fingertips brushed the controls and he zoomed in on the spot. "An abandoned duradium mine—the metal would block any sensor scans. Good eye, Stringer."

"We should move on to the next recording," Zib suggested.

The screen changed again, this time to a shot of a desert planet. The assembled Heroes could hear Stormer's voice on the speakers.

Mission Log, Stormer recording. When a Hero goes bad, he's the worst of criminals. Not only does he know all the secrets of Hero Factory, but in the end, any damage he does is our responsibility. We built him. We trained him. It's up to us to stop him.

It was hot. Stormer's internal sensors had already triggered his armor's automatic cooling system. Normally, changes in temperature did not affect his systems, but the heat on this particular world was so intense that sometimes even weapons malfunctioned.

He had been here more often than he wanted to remember. It was a small planet in a backwater part of the galaxy, not even important enough to have been given a name. Its year-round population was maybe a few hundred, but at any given time, there might be a thousand or more robots passing through. The place had no government, no courts, and no local law enforcement, and its only industry was crime. More accurately, it was a place criminals on the run or in between jobs could come to hide, rest, refit, or sell their stolen goods.

In other words, it was the perfect place to look for Core Hunter.

Stormer had particularly bitter memories of this villain. The two had fought once before. Stormer had been partnered with a rookie, and Core Hunter took the young Hero's core. Stormer came to the rescue with a replacement, but Core Hunter used the distraction to get away.

Apparently, business was slow for Core Hunter these days. He had resorted to simple robbery, raiding a string of mansions on a resort world a light-year away. Oddly enough, he had done a lot of damage but taken very little. Most of the valuable items were found abandoned not far from the scenes of the crimes, but the one thing he had escaped with was an artifact of seemingly not much worth. It was a piece of a larger item, that much was clear, but what that item might be was unknown.

Stormer made doubly sure all the security systems were set on the Hero craft before walking into the nearest town. He headed right for the heart of the place: the refueling center. This was where deals got done on a crime planet like this.

The robot behind the counter was named Geb. He had started out as a cleaner and took over the station when the previous owner accidentally fell down the stairs — twice — and had to be deactivated. As soon as his optic sensors registered Stormer, he started polishing everything in sight in an effort to look busy.

"Morning, Geb," said Stormer. "How's business?"

"Quiet, Mr. Stormer," Geb answered hurriedly.

"Real quiet. I've never seen the place so dead. I doubt you'll find anything—or anyone—you're looking for here."

Stormer looked around. The room was full of robots. A few were in sleep mode, but the rest were all keeping an eye on him with a hand on their weapons.

"I can see that," he said, turning back to Geb. "Well, I didn't really expect this to be a profitable visit. You wouldn't do business with a big-timer like Core Hunter, right?"

Geb stopped polishing for about a quarter of a second. Then he resumed, doing it twice as fast as before.

"Because you know what I would do to you if you *were* doing business with him," Stormer continued, his voice dropping low. "As a representative of Hero Factory, I would have to shut this place down. That would give you time to pay Makuhero City a visit—a very *long* visit, if you get my meaning."

Geb chuckled nervously. "Heh. Like I would be stupid enough to let a most-wanted type like

Core Hunter use my place. Why, he would insist on using the spare room — the one upstairs and to the left — and want me to screen anyone who came up to see him."

The robot looked quickly from side to side, then leaned in close and said to Stormer, "I mean, who has time to do that? I have a business to run here. Anyone could slip right past me and go upstairs. Understand?"

Stormer nodded and started for the staircase. He was intercepted about halfway there by a robot about twice his height with a badly damaged face and some exposed wiring on his left arm. He blocked Stormer and growled, "You're that Hero, aren't you?"

"That's right," Stormer replied.

"You broke up a robbery last year and threw my whole gang in jail."

Stormer braced himself for a fight, remembering that he didn't have a friend in the place. "Do you want to join them?"

To Stormer's surprise, the big robot smiled and clapped a large hand on his shoulder. "Nah.

I never liked those guys anyway. Just wanted to say thanks."

The Alpha Team leader continued for the stairs, thinking about what a very weird place this planet without a name could be.

The door to the spare room was locked. Stormer kicked it in. The room wasn't much to look at. There was one window that looked out on the street, four bare walls, and two chairs. Propped against one of the chairs was an old-fashioned communications tablet. As Stormer watched, its screen flashed, "5 . . . 4 . . . 3 . . . 2 . . . 1 . . ."

The Hero didn't hesitate. Just as the count-down reached zero, he leapt through the window. Behind him, there was a blinding flash and a sizzle of electricity.

Stormer rolled in midair and landed on his feet in the dust. He glanced back up at the scene of his narrow escape. Core Hunter was clever — he had planted a device in the room, probably affixed to the ceiling, that could overload a Hero Core. If Stormer hadn't gotten out when he did, his power would have been extinguished completely.

Core Hunter knew there would be a Hero on his trail, thought Stormer. *That's why he set the trap. But he would want to be nearby to watch it work. So where . . . ?*

The Hero looked up and down the street. His eye alighted on a second-floor window in a building across the street from the refueling station. It would be the perfect vantage point to watch goings-on in the rigged room. If Core Hunter was in there, he would know Stormer had escaped his trap. Had he booby-trapped the building he was hiding in as well?

Not all of it, I'm guessing, Stormer thought with a smile.

He made a show of shrugging and then stalking off down the street, as if frustrated that his target had eluded him. He kept right on going out of town, got back into his Hero craft, and took off. To anyone watching, it would look like he was heading off-world.

Stormer piloted the ship directly over Core Hunter's hideout. Then he slammed the "Eject" button. The ship's canopy popped off and he was launched into the sky. Angling his fall, he aimed right for the roof of the target building. An instant later, he crashed through the roof and into Core Hunter's room. The villain jumped to his feet, startled.

"You're getting sloppy in your old age, CH," said Stormer, thrusting with his ice blade. "You forgot to guard the approach from above."

"Maybe I just wanted to see if you are still the same old Stormer." Core Hunter snarled, evading the blow. "Haven't they upgraded you yet?"

"For an amateur like you? It would be a waste of resources." Stormer laughed. "Hand over what you stole and surrender. You know how this is going to end."

Core Hunter smiled savagely in response, already powering up his weapon. It was designed for one purpose only: to remove Hero Cores intact.

"What I stole is where you won't find it, not unless Zib is building robot dune dragons now," said the villain. "As for how this is going to end,

I don't think I'll stop with taking your Hero Core. I think I'll mount your armor in the refueling station so I can do all my deals right in front of you from now on."

Stormer raised his sword above his head, as if about to plunge it down toward Core Hunter. The villain raised his own weapon to block the strike. In that moment, Stormer stabbed the sword into the floor, then swung himself around it to deliver a solid kick to Core Hunter. The villain staggered back against the wall.

"A decoy move," said Core Hunter. "Real cute."

"If you think that's cute, this one is downright adorable," said Stormer, advancing on his foe.

With blinding speed, Core Hunter raised his weapon, and it latched on to Stormer's Hero Core. The villain smiled, anticipating the moment he would yank it out and Stormer would go down like a felled tree.

For his part, Stormer showed no sign of panic. He unclipped a small piece of metal from his hip and slapped it onto Core Hunter's weapon.

"A little gift from the weapons crew at Hero Factory — they say hi."

A massive jolt of electricity shot from the small device into Core Hunter's weapon, traveling through it to stun the villain. By the time Core Hunter regained his senses, he was Stormer's prisoner.

"Go ahead, lock me up," said Core Hunter as Stormer led him outside to his now hovering Hero craft. "But I'll get out again, and when I do, I'll have the power to grind Hero Factory into dust."

"You won't be getting out," Stormer answered. "Nobody breaks out of Hero Factory."

Core Hunter grinned. "Then I guess I better make sure I won't be going there."

Sparks suddenly shot out from Core Hunter's shoulders, elbows, and knees. The villain's legs buckled even as he began to laugh, a laugh that grew harsher and more mechanical sounding as he sagged to the ground. Before Stormer could check to see what was wrong with his captive, Core Hunter's metal body exploded.

The force of the blast sent Stormer flying through the front wall of an abandoned building and out the back. After he pulled himself up out of the dust, it took him a moment to clear his head. By the time he made it back to the street, all that was left of Core Hunter was red-hot, twisted metal.

"I . . . don't buy it," Stormer said as he looked down at the ruin. "He wouldn't shut himself down just to avoid prison. I—"

Stormer's questions were interrupted by the buzzing of his communicator. He hit the "Talk" button and said, "Stormer here."

"How nice," came the reply. The voice belonged to Core Hunter. "I bet you wish I was there with you. And, yes, I do still remember all those special Hero Factory radio frequencies."

"Okay, so how did you pull this off?" asked Stormer.

"Simple." Core Hunter chuckled. "A long time ago, in Makuhero City, someone made a robot who turned out to be me. I thought that was such a good idea that I made another one. It's been very handy being able to send him to places that might not be . . . healthy for the real me. And if he ever got into real trouble—well, ka-boom."

Stormer looked around. Was Core Hunter nearby? Was he about to spring an ambush?

"I'm sure you're scanning the rooftops for me by now," Core Hunter said. "Don't bother. I'm nowhere near that dust bowl of a planet. I hope you enjoyed the welcome I arranged for you, or one of your kind, anyway, just in case someone came looking for me."

"I'm still looking for you," Stormer said coldly. "And I will find you."

"Unless I find you first, old friend," Core Hunter replied. "Think about that."

The communicator went dead. Wherever he was, Core Hunter had signed off.

The recording ended there. Any other Hero might have been embarrassed to have his colleagues see him getting tricked like that. But

Stormer didn't have time to worry about such things, not with the galaxy in danger.

"So what do you think?" asked Breez. "Where did he hide it?"

"Not there," said Stormer. "Core Hunter was never on that planet. He sent his double there, with orders to get noticed. If anybody found his trail, they would eventually hear he was on that world and walk into his trap."

"Then we didn't learn much from this," said Bulk.

"Sure we did," said Furno. "We learned where the thing *isn't*."

The screen blazed to life again. This time, it was Stringer's voice everyone heard.

Mission Log, Stringer reporting. Our old pal Core Hunter has trapped himself this time. I was in the sector when I got a report of his latest robbery. I chased him in my Hero craft until he had to dock with an old cargo freighter adrift in space. He's in here somewhere . . . just have to track him down.

Stringer moved slowly and quietly through the narrow corridors of the freighter. The only illumination came from emergency lights high up on the walls, which cast a ghostly glow on everything. Stringer wondered how many centuries they had been burning.

So far, he had stumbled across a half dozen of the crew. The robots weren't dead, but they weren't functioning either. As far as he could tell, they still had power, but each one was totally unresponsive. It was like they had been shocked into suspended animation.

The ship didn't seem too badly damaged. There was certainly no sign of an asteroid strike or anything like that. The only really odd thing he had run across was some deep scoring along the bottom of a few of the exterior walls, as if something was using them to sharpen its claws.

Stringer took out his sensor pack. If the whole crew was in sleep mode, there should be only one other life sign on board beside himself, and that would be Core Hunter. He flipped the scanner switch and waited.

It took only a few seconds for the sensor to sweep the entire vast ship. Sure enough, it picked up Core Hunter's energy . . . but it also picked up something else. It was something mechanical, but not a standard robot. The power readings seemed all wrong, but one thing was clear: Whatever it was, it was on the move. The signal was traveling impossibly fast, heading for a junction up ahead that would put it midway between Core Hunter and Stringer.

"Okay," whispered Stringer. "Let's see just what you are."

The Hero slipped through the hallways until he was close to where the signal had come to a stop. The lights were starting to burn out here, flashing on and off so that it looked like lightning bolts were striking inside the ship. Stringer shifted his optics to maximum to try to catch a glimpse of the source of the strange energies.

And, suddenly, there it was: a flash of metallic wings, a gnarled face with a mouth full of jagged teeth, claws that extended at least half a meter in length. Then the lights shut off and he was swallowed by the darkness.

Whew, thought Stringer. *Why do I think I just saw what shocked this whole crew to sleep?*

The lights flashed on. The thing had vanished.

Stringer glanced down at his sensor. There was a little Hero Factory icon rotating on the screen, indicating that the device was recalibrating. It was a process that took only seconds, but it felt like hours. Finally, the main screen reappeared. There was Stringer's signal, and Core Hunter's still some distance away, and there was the creature's . . .

Right behind Stringer.

The Hero whirled. The creature lashed out with a spindly arm, its claw knocking the sensor pack out of Stringer's hand. It fell to the ground and smashed to pieces.

Stringer powered up his sonic blaster and fired. To his amazement, though, it had no effect. The creature just darted forward, its big eyes fixed on the Hero, wings beating rapidly. Stringer stumbled backward, ready to fend off the attack.

There was a flash of light down the left-hand corridor, then another and another. The creature turned in that direction, then flew off to investigate. Stringer, it had apparently decided, could wait.

The Hero allowed himself a sigh of relief. It

would be a long time before he would be able to forget those eyes locked in on him, and . . .

Something clicked into place in Stringer's central processor then. The creature had huge eyes, and probably amazing eyesight—but the Hero had not seen any kind of an audio receptor anywhere on it. No wonder a sonic attack had done no good—the thing was deaf!

"Well, that's just great," he muttered to himself.

"Yes, isn't it?"

Stringer turned to see Core Hunter standing behind him, his energy blaster aimed right at the Hero. He was trapped. It would be impossible to make a move without Core Hunter striking him down.

"Hey, don't you think we have a bigger problem right now than me against you?" said Stringer.

"No kidding," the villain replied. "Why do you think I tossed those magnesium flares?"

"You—?"

"Once it gets you, I will be next on the list," said Core Hunter. "Seems to me we should be working together to stop it."

Stringer frowned. Core Hunter was nasty, treacherous, and an overall creep. He was also right. It would be a lot easier to stop the creature without having to look out for an attack from behind all the time.

"Okay, I'll work with you," the Hero said. "But don't expect me to shake your hand."

"I don't do hands," Core Hunter answered, smiling. "I do cores."

Stringer knelt and poked through the shattered remains of his sensor pack. "Any idea how we find it again?"

"It will find us, don't worry. We're the only other things moving on this tub. It's a hunter. That's what it does."

Stringer made some adjustments to his armor. If the creature couldn't hear, then the best weapon would be subsonics — sounds too low to be heard normally. The vibrations would be enough to do some damage.

"So, any idea where that thing came from?" asked Core Hunter. "I haven't been in the Hero Factory database in a while—"

"I wonder why," Stringer cut in.

Core Hunter ignored the jibe. "Don't you guys usually track the big winged monsters of the universe?"

"Usually," said Stringer. "I guess we missed this one. But I have an idea of where to look."

Stringer started running. Core Hunter, no longer getting the kind of regular training Hero Factory personnel did, had to struggle to keep up.

"Where are we going?"

"When I did my sensor sweep, I spotted something that had to be the main cargo hold," said Stringer. "Bet our pal came from in there."

"Why not just from outer space?"

Stringer shook his head. "Only two ways in: rip your way through the hull, which means explosive decompression and the whole crew gets sucked out into the vacuum, or make it past multiple air locks. I doubt the robots that ran this ship would have waited patiently while that thing cycled through the different chambers on its way in."

Core Hunter had to agree. "Somebody shipped it, then . . . and it broke loose."

They had reached the central cargo bay by now. As Stringer expected, the hatch had been torn open a long, long time ago. Cautiously, he stepped into the vast, dark room. Behind him, he heard Core Hunter chuckle.

"I'm surprised you went first," said the villain.

"I'm Hero Factory," Stringer answered. "We always go first."

It took quite a while to search the hold and find what they were looking for. The crate was way in the back, mostly shattered. Stringer was able to read the cargo number on one of the panels. None of the computer terminals still had power, but Core Hunter made a lucky find: a list of cargo created the old-fashioned way, on a piece of paper.

"Found it," Core Hunter said after a moment. "XJC-360014. It was legitimate cargo from the outer rim of the galaxy . . . but it says here it was an infant."

Stringer gestured to the ruined door. "I guess they grow up fast around here."

Core Hunter suddenly held up a hand. "Did you hear that?"

Stringer had. Sound was his business, and even the smallest noise would catch his attention. This one was the scrape of metal claws on a metal floor. The thing was coming their way.

"Hide!" he whispered.

The two robots took cover. A moment later, the creature appeared in the doorway, wings slowly moving back and forth. It sniffed the air.

I should have known better than to trust someone from Hero Factory, Core Hunter was surely thinking. *Stringer has led us right to this thing's nest! Best thing to do is let it have the Hero while I make a run for my ship.*

Core Hunter is going to run, thought Stringer. *But maybe I can use that to my advantage — just a matter of getting him to run the right way.*

Stringer took aim with his sonic blaster, but not at the creature. Instead, he zeroed in on a stack of crates off to Core Hunter's right. One good shot of sonic waves brought the whole pile crashing down.

Everything happened fast then. The creature's keen eyes caught the sight of the crates falling and it turned in that direction. Core Hunter took off running to his left, which meant crossing in front of the main door. Stringer waited until just the right moment, then unleashed another blast. This one hit Core Hunter broadside and sent him flying like a missile right into the creature.

The impact was jarring, sending both villain and monster crashing into and through the wall of the corridor. Stringer was on his feet, racing for the door, already powering up for another attack.

Before he could reach his targets, Core Hunter came flying out of the darkness right at him. He was followed by a very angry creature.

Core Hunter did a flip in midair, so that he hit the wall with his feet and could push himself off for a semi-perfect landing in the corridor. "Thanks for the warning before," he growled.

"Well, I figured since you were on your way out anyway, maybe you could knock something down for me."

The creature lashed out with its right wing. The blow was so powerful that, even though it didn't connect, the breeze alone was enough to stagger Stringer.

"I've had enough of this," snapped Core Hunter. He started rapidly firing energy bursts at the creature, each one hitting with the force of a pile driver. The creature was driven back against the bulkhead.

Stringer expected the monster to roar in anger or howl in pain. The last thing he expected was what he saw and heard: The beast was crying.

"Hunter, knock it off," Stringer said. When the barrage continued, he turned and hit the villain with a blast of high-pitched ultrasonics, just enough to get his attention. "I mean it!"

"What is wrong with you?!" Core Hunter yelled. "I thought we were trying to stop this thing!"

"Yeah," said Stringer. "I thought so, too."

The Hero slowly approached the beast and laid a hand on its shoulder. At first, it shied away, but after a moment the creature just sagged against the wall. It seemed in no mood to keep fighting.

"What are you waiting for? Kill it!" shouted Core Hunter.

"We're idiots," said Stringer. "Totally dumb."

"Talk sense."

Stringer turned from the beast to look at his temporary ally. "It was shipped here as cargo, remember? It was a baby, who burst out of its crate and found itself on this ship. What do you think it wanted most? I'm guessing it was looking for the way home."

"You're too sentimental." Core Hunter snarled. "You're going to get us smashed to bits."

Stringer kept his hand firmly on the beast, and his comforting eyes locked on its pleading ones. He was doing his best to project calm and reassurance. "No, it all makes sense. It tore its way out of the cargo hold—interior doors on freighters aren't that thick—and then it tried to get off the ship. I saw deep scratches along the bottom of the exterior walls. It was trying to claw its way out."

Core Hunter was beginning to understand. "But exterior walls are reinforced two or three times. It must not have been strong enough to get out."

"Right. And since it failed as a 'child,' it stopped trying. It would probably be strong enough now to tear the ship apart, if it wanted to."

"How do we keep it from wanting to?"

Stringer looked at Core Hunter. "We give it what it wants."

It took a long time and a lot of patience to coax the creature into following the two robots. Stringer and Core Hunter led it to the nearest air lock. "You'll have to work the controls, and I'll guide it through," said Stringer. "It trusts me."

"Obviously, it hasn't had any dealings with Hero Factory before," said Core Hunter. "All right, let's make this fast. I'm a professional criminal, not a babysitter for monsters."

At Stringer's signal, Core Hunter went to work, opening first one air lock, then closing it and opening the next, and so on. One by one, Stringer and the creature moved through them, each time making it that much closer to open space.

Soon, they had reached the very last hatch. Stringer knew this was where things would get dangerous. Core Hunter had to keep the previous air lock open long enough for Stringer to make it back, or the Hero would be sucked out into space. Even if he avoided that fate, it was possible the creature would react to his departure by turning back and pursuing him. If it did, and started tearing through the air locks, everyone on the ship was doomed.

Stringer gave the beast a gentle push toward the last hatch, then turned around to head back into the ship. To his shock, he saw the air lock door was closed behind him — Core Hunter had trapped him!

Before he could react, the lights on the outer hatch had gone from red to yellow to green. The hatch slid open. The creature unfurled its wings and flew out into open space as if it had been doing so all its life. But Stringer was pulled violently out of the ship, helpless to the freezing cold of the interstellar void.

There was no hope, he knew that. No other Hero Factory ship was close enough to come to his rescue in time. In a matter of moments, his mechanisms would freeze, his Hero Core would short out, and he would be gone forever.

And then an amazing thing happened.

The creature looked back over its shoulder and saw Stringer. It made a wide arc and turned back, flying toward the one who had freed it. Scooping Stringer up in its arms, it flew back toward the ship. When it got close, it suddenly veered to the right and headed for Core Hunter's ship, docked at the freighter.

With one swipe of its metallic wings, it tore a hole in the side of the small vessel. Then it carefully shoved Stringer into Core Hunter's ship. The Hero had to hang on desperately to keep from being pulled out through the gash in the hull, but with difficulty, he managed to crawl to the air lock connecting Core Hunter's ship to the freighter. Once the outer hatch opened, Stringer was able to get inside and close it behind him. He was safe.

He would never see the creature again, and could only hope it somehow found its way home, wherever in the galaxy that might be. As for Core Hunter, he had vanished, having stolen Stringer's Hero craft.

But I am pretty sure I will be seeing him again, Stringer thought to himself at the time.

"Stealing Stringer's ship was Core Hunter's big mistake," said Stormer. He looked at the newer members of Alpha Team. "Tell me why."

"Each ship has a homing beacon," said Breez. "So we could track him."

"And?" prompted Stormer.

"Auto-control," said Furno. "Those earlier models could be controlled remotely from Hero Factory. One touch of a button—"

"And he flew straight to jail." Stringer smiled.

"Unfortunately, he had no pieces of stolen property with him when he was arrested," said Stormer. "Stringer, what about the third piece?"

Stringer shrugged. "His ship was clean. He could have stashed it on the freighter, but it would have to be hidden really well—we searched from bow to stern."

"Where's the freighter now?" asked Bulk.

"Crew got revived, cargo got off-loaded, and it wound up in a ship graveyard in the center of the galaxy, with all the rest of the junk," said Stringer.

He turned to a wall terminal and punched in some numbers. An image of the freighter appeared on the screen. "Registry check says it's still there."

Stormer nodded. "Okay, we split into three teams. We'll cover all three locations as closely as possible. If Core Hunter shows up, alert Hero Factory immediately."

The Alpha Team leader looked out over his assembled Heroes. "Those three logs you just watched had one thing in common: overconfident

Heroes who let a dangerous criminal get away. We *cannot* allow that to happen again. This time, there is no margin for error."

"I still don't understand," said Furno. "What are those things, and why are they such a threat?"

"According to everything Hero Factory has been able to find out, those three items — when put together — will make a weapon of unimaginable power," said Stormer. "Those of us in this room are the only hope of stopping that from happening.

"We get it right," he finished, "or we don't come back."

5

Core Hunter checked his star charts for the third time. He knew he wouldn't have much time to do what he had to, and there were no spare moments for mistakes. Hero Factory had been wounded by the mass breakout from their own prison and the Heroes were reacting just as he expected they would: with full force, in an all-out effort to recapture the escapees.

So far, he had managed to evade the net. Part of this was skill, part luck, and part trickery — he had pointed a few villains in the direction of criminal "sure things," only to have them walk right into the hands of Hero Factory. This kept the Heroes busy while he made his preparations.

He wondered how much Stormer and the others knew by now. Were they concerned at all about why he had stolen the things he did years ago, or why the items were never recovered? Did they imagine he would go back for them again? Or were they totally in the dark, waiting for him to pull another robbery or hunt another Hero?

Core Hunter laughed. They would be waiting a long time, if so. He was done with little jobs, done with taking revenge on Hero Factory. When this job was done, he would be the undisputed ruler of the galaxy, and Stormer would be polishing his armor for him.

He punched a course into his navigational computer, set the autopilot, and leaned back to watch the stars go by. Around each of those specks of light were planets, and on many of them there were intelligent beings . . . and not one of those beings knew what was about to happen, or that everything they knew was about to change forever.

Power, he decided, had its appeal—but the anticipation of getting power was almost as sweet.

Bulk banked the ship and brought it in for a landing on the desert sands. Stormer had decided it made no sense to send the veterans back to where they had originally fought Core Hunter, so they switched up destinations. Bulk was sent to where Stormer had battled the fake villain.

Breez sat next to him, looking somewhat uncomfortable. She didn't like deserts. Much of her tactical training so far had centered on finding cover and staging ambushes. In a place like this, there was no cover and your enemy could see you coming from a hundred miles away.

"Do you think Geb is still on this planet?" she asked. "Maybe he's moved on."

Bulk shook his head. "Geb is a small-time criminal," he replied. "His type doesn't move on from a safe spot—too dangerous out there."

The two Heroes left the ship. They were going

in disguised as duradium smugglers and had even abandoned the Hero craft for this mission. Bulk had been flying an old cargo ship someone had reconditioned to carry "extra" goods. It flew like a brick, and probably a pilot with less skill than Bulk would never have gotten it off the ground, let alone off-planet.

They walked perfectly side by side toward Geb's establishment. Real smugglers never get too far ahead of each other, for fear of what might go on behind their backs.

"Remember the plan?" said Bulk.

Breez nodded. "It seems awfully . . . simple."

"Simple works," said Bulk. "Simple doesn't make them think too hard."

They walked into Geb's place. It was crowded. That was a good thing. Geb would be distracted by the noise and commotion and wouldn't be listening too hard to what was being said to him. Bulk and Breez walked up to the counter.

"Hi," said Bulk. "I'm looking for someone named Geb."

"I'm Geb." Nodding toward Breez, the station owner said, "Who's your friend?"

Bulk leaned in close. "I wouldn't look directly at her. The last robot that did that . . . well, they're still trying to put him back together, if you know what I mean. If she didn't know where the mine was, I'd never travel with her."

"Mine?" Geb replied. "What mine?"

"Sshhhh!" hissed Bulk. "I thought you were someone I could trust."

"Oh, I am, I am!" Geb insisted. "Ask anyone."

"Because if you're not . . ." Bulk began, inclining his head a little toward Breez. Taking the hint, she gave a low growl.

Seeing that Geb looked appropriately nervous, Bulk reached into his belt and produced a small chunk of duradium. After making a show of ensuring no one was watching, he showed it to Geb. "There's more where this came from. But, for now, I need a place to stash it. I have a buyer flying in day after tomorrow, and I don't want to carry it around with me . . . you understand."

"I can hide it for you," Geb whispered. "I know just the place."

Bulk smiled. "And I'm sure you'll take good care of it. But my partner likes to see things for herself. So why don't you show us your hiding spot, and then we can celebrate our good fortune?"

Geb hesitated for just a fraction of a second. He had to know there was a risk in doing what Bulk asked, but he also knew the duradium was real. If there was more of it, and if he could negotiate a fee for keeping the merchandise safe, well, that was worth a little risk . . . wasn't it?

"Okay, okay," said Geb. "Come with me."

Geb led them into a back room, then through a secret door in the wall to a smaller chamber. Once inside, he pulled open a trapdoor and they descended underground into a crudely dug pit. At the bottom of the hole was a metal crate. Geb produced an old-fashioned metal key and opened it.

Bulk looked inside. Sure enough, there was the item Core Hunter had stolen years before. The villain had pulled a double bluff. He had entrusted the stolen loot to a duplicate of himself that he posted here. When the fake was inevitably exposed, everyone would think the real Core Hunter had never been here and so what he stole couldn't be, either.

From here, it should be simple, Bulk said to himself. He and Breez would sneak back here at night, pry open the crate, and reclaim what Core Hunter had hidden. Without that one piece, he wouldn't be able to reassemble the box and use it as a weapon. Problem solved.

Bulk turned to Geb. "Looks like we have a deal."

"Great," said Geb. "Then I'll just—"

Before Geb could finish his sentence, he suddenly shot straight up out of the hole, smashing through the ceiling of the room above and on through the roof of the building itself. Bulk and Breez started to climb out of the hole, only to find they were staring up at Core Hunter.

"Geb never was too bright," said the villain. "But he really should have known to stay exclusive to one client. Anyway, he's where he always wanted to be now—way up on top."

"What did you do to him?" demanded Breez.

"Little something I've been working on," Core Hunter answered. "An anti-grav disk—works like this."

He threw a second disk down into the hole. It hit the crate, which immediately began to rise rapidly into the air. Core Hunter caught it as it went by, extracted his item, and then let the crate keep sailing into the sky.

"Now, what do I do about you two? I could just leave you buried down there, I guess. Or I could take you as hostages, though Bulk would probably be pretty heavy to lug around everywhere."

"Why don't I save you the trouble of deciding?" Bulk snarled, launching a rocket from his weapon.

Core Hunter had no chance to dodge. But to Bulk's shock, a hooded figure suddenly appeared and slammed into the villain, allowing him to avoid the rocket. The projectile struck the ceiling and detonated, raining wood and stone down upon Bulk and Breez.

"Okay," said Core Hunter, scrambling to his feet. "Burying you it is, then."

He turned to the hooded robot who had saved him. "Not that I'm complaining, but what was in that rescue for you? If you think I'm going to share . . . well, anything, you're mistaken."

"I do not want anything from you," said the figure. "Merely that you continue your quest. You must gather all three pieces of the box, before Hero Factory can stop you."

"Wow, really? Here I was planning to just sit around until they arrested me." Core Hunter sneered. "Is that all you wanted to say?"

The hooded robot shook his head. "Two more things: The piece hidden in the duradium mine is in serious jeopardy; and your enemies are about to free themselves."

Core Hunter glanced back at where he had left Bulk and Breez, just as the pile of rubble exploded upward. That was followed by the emergence of two very angry Heroes. The villain turned back to his new ally, only to find the strange robot gone.

Breez saw the hooded one disappear, but

didn't care—her target was Core Hunter, and she was flying right for him.

It was too late for Bulk to shout a warning, but he knew she was in terrible danger. He unleashed a barrage of rockets at Core Hunter, driving the villain back toward the main room of the refueling station.

"What are you doing?" Breez shouted. "I had him!"

"He was about to have you, rookie," Bulk growled. "As soon as you got close enough, he would have taken your Hero Core."

The two Heroes charged after Core Hunter. They found him among the crowd in the refueling center. As soon as they appeared, Core Hunter pointed at them. "I've got a big, fat reward for whoever stops those Heroes!"

Three dozen robots rose as one. They would have gladly pounded on Heroes just for the fun of it, but throw a reward in, and the only question was whether they would fight one another to be the first to get to Breez and Bulk.

"What do we do?" asked Breez.

"What do you think?" Bulk answered. "We fight our way out of here!"

The two robots waded into the sea of enemies. For the next fifteen minutes, the only sounds were the clang of metal on metal as the battle raged. By the time it was over, neither Geb's station nor any of its customers were still standing.

"Are you all right?" Bulk asked his partner.

"Right arm's a little banged up," Breez replied. "I'm sure Zib can fix it when we get back to Hero Factory."

Bulk looked up and down the street. "Core Hunter's long gone. He got what he wanted here. It's up to the others now."

Breez nodded, troubled. "I'd like to know who that was that saved Core Hunter, and how he managed to disappear."

"Whoever he was, we'll meet again," Bulk vowed. "Count on it."

6

Stormer yanked hard on the controls of the Hero craft, throwing the ship into a violent right bank. Outside, bright blue bolts of energy flew by, some coming close enough to sear the hull.

"Initiating evasive maneuvers," said Stormer. "Hang on!"

"Why are they shooting at us?" demanded Furno. "We're the good guys!"

"System's automated," Stormer answered, eyes locked on the sensor screen. "Good guys, bad guys, it's all the same to them."

Stormer threw the ship into a sudden roll, just barely avoiding a spread of missiles. Furno, who was still fumbling with his straps, had to grab on to his chair to keep from being plastered against the ceiling. Once the ship righted itself, he slapped the communications controls and yelled, "This is Hero craft One, repeat, Hero craft One. Cease firing, we are officers of the law!"

"You're wasting your time, rookie," said Stormer. "Don't worry, I know what to do. I've been here before."

Furno could see the spaceport on the sensor screen, looking like a big green blob. All around it were red dots, representing the sources of the antispacecraft fire zeroed in on the Hero craft. The young Hero expected Stormer to make a conventional, if ultra-fast, landing approach, doing his best to dodge the blaster fire. But Stormer had something else in mind.

As they neared the spaceport, Stormer pulled back on the stick, causing the ship to gain altitude. When they were as high as they could go without leaving the atmosphere, he suddenly threw the craft into a tight corkscrew maneuver, spiraling down toward the landing field.

Furno held on to whatever he could grab and watched as the ground rapidly rose up to meet them. Hero craft were built for speed and maneuverability, but not this kind of a stunt. He could hear the metal of the hull groaning from the strain.

Just before they were about to crash, Stormer yanked hard on the controls, leveling the ship off, and skidded it into a landing. As soon as they had stopped, Stormer opened the hatch and said, "Come on."

Furno followed, wary of a possible ambush. After all, this planet was supposed to be just a big bank, but he had seen military-run worlds that didn't have that much firepower protecting them. There had been nothing in Bulk's log about this kind of a reception.

As if he had read Furno's mind, Stormer said, "There have been a lot of changes since Bulk was here. Core Hunter robbing the place was an embarrassment. They weren't about to let anything like that happen again. So they beefed up security . . . a lot."

"So what if they nail Core Hunter's ship on the way in? Mission's over, then, right?"

"We're Hero Factory," Stormer replied. "Things are never that easy."

As they traveled to the mine, Furno ran over what he knew about duradium. In its refined state, it was one of the more valuable minerals in the galaxy, used to make highly conductive wiring for machinery. Raw, duradium was one of the more dangerous things to mine, because exposure to it weakened metals to the point where they crumbled. For that reason, active duradium mines required massive numbers of robot miners who worked in a series of limited shifts. No miner was allowed to dig for more than an hour at a time.

The mine on this particular planet had been abandoned years ago. There was still duradium in it, but the expense and difficulty involved with getting it out made it no longer worthwhile to the locals. There was much more money to be made as the galaxy's bank than as one more mining world.

"Hey, I just thought of something," said Furno. "If Core Hunter hid what he stole in the mine, wouldn't it have crumbled to dust by now?"

"Sure," said Stormer. "If it's made of a metal we know, and if it isn't shielded somehow . . . and if Core Hunter were stupid. And, unfortunately, we know that last one isn't true."

"So what's the plan?"

"Core Hunter didn't have a lot of time to hide it, which means it can't be that far inside the mine. If he hasn't shown up yet, we take it and go. If he's already here, well . . . we take him, too."

Those last few words came out in a tone Furno had only heard a time or two before. It usually meant someone was in a lot of trouble.

The mine entrance was in the side of a mountain. It was sealed with a high-density plastic that wouldn't be affected by the duradium and was strong enough to keep most intruders out. But Furno knew it wouldn't stop Core Hunter, and it wasn't going to stop Hero Factory, either.

"There's no time to ask for official permission to open this," said Stormer. He detached a small metal square from his hip and placed it on the barrier. "Find cover."

The two Heroes ducked behind a boulder. A few seconds later, the barrier shattered like a piece of glass that had just met a rock.

"Where can I get one of those little metal things?" asked Furno, impressed.

"Ask Zib. He probably has a few lying around. Let's go."

It was pitch-black in the mine. Both Heroes switched on belt lights. Their illumination revealed that the mine must have been closed abruptly, because there were still tools and equipment scattered about, even robot fuel cells and other valuable items. The coating of dust on the floor of the mine said that no one had been inside in years.

"At least we beat Core Hunter here," said Furno. "Let's get what we need and get out of this place."

"Something's . . . wrong," said Stormer. He flashed his light along the ceiling and the walls and floor. "I'm not sure what, but . . . Furno, scan the dust."

"Scan the—?"

"Just do it."

Furno swept his sensor pack over the floor. Then he did it a second time. "This doesn't make any sense, Stormer. This isn't rock dust, or plant pollen, or anything else natural—it's all chemicals of one kind or another."

Stormer glanced at the sensor screen. "It's fake dust. Someone's been here recently and doesn't want us to know about it. Three guesses who."

"But the barrier on the mine entrance was active," countered Furno.

Stormer shook his head. "There are a lot of ways to take down a barrier . . . and put one back up. Core Hunter expected us to figure out where he had to have hidden the piece, and to show up here."

Furno was now facing the mine entrance, with his sensor pack going wild. "We have to get out of here! I've got multiple energy surges near the entrance and—"

The world suddenly exploded. Stormer and Furno were hurled backward by the force of the blast. The air was filled with choking dust by the falling ominous rocks and tons of earth.

Stormer forced himself to get to his hands and knees. The incredible noise had temporarily knocked his audio receptors offline and his optics were recalibrating to see through the smoke and dust. Furno, who had been closer to the blast, was still on his back on the ground. A closer examination revealed that the rookie's systems were rebooting.

A sensor scan confirmed the bad news: There were a few tons of stone and dirt between them and the outside. If there was another exit from the mine, sensors couldn't pick it up—not surprising, since duradium blocked most scans.

Furno abruptly sat up. "How much trouble are we in?"

"Enough," said Stormer. "Are you fit for action?"

Furno stood up. "What's the plan?"

"I can blast us out of here, but not without bringing the rest of the ceiling down on top of us. We need to shore up the walls with beams, and we need to do it in less than an hour. Otherwise, the duradium is going to do nasty things to every part of us that's made of metal."

The Heroes got to work. Furno ventured deeper into the mine and tore beams free from spots that seemed they could spare them. Then he dragged the timber back to where Stormer was waiting. Stormer would lift them and jam them into place in an effort to reinforce the walls and ceiling as much as possible. Meanwhile, time was ticking away.

With two minutes left, Stormer told Furno to stop working and get ready to run as soon as the way out was clear. He raised his weapon, aimed, mentally triggered the blast—

And nothing happened.

Fighting to stay calm, Stormer examined his weapon. It didn't take long to find the problem: The duradium had already corroded some of the metallic wiring that ran from the firing mechanism to the housing. In other words, he was now carrying a useless piece of junk.

"Furno, it's up to you!" he shouted. "My weapon's down — blast the rocks!"

It was risky. Where Stormer could have just blown the boulders to pieces, Furno's plasma weapon would superheat them. Done right, the rocks would be vaporized. Use too little power and they would turn into molten magma and the Heroes wouldn't need duradium exposure to be destroyed.

Furno fired. The bolt of plasma struck the rocks blocking the entrance. There was a hiss and the sudden smell of scorched earth. Then the stone vanished as if it had never been there, and the way out was clear.

Well, almost clear.

As Stormer and Furno emerged from the mine, they found themselves facing the weapons of a half dozen security robots.

"I am Sentinel Mechanoid 411. You are under arrest for trespassing in a restricted area and destruction of private property. You will please not resist. Thank you."

"Well, at least they're polite," said Furno.

"We don't have time for this," Stormer said, sounding exhausted and fed up. "Listen, 411, or whatever your number is—we're Hero Factory on a vital mission. You are interfering with our duties. Stand down."

"You are under arrest for trespassing in a restricted area and destruction of private property," 411 repeated. "You will please—"

Stormer took three quick steps forward, lifted 411 in the air, and threw him two hundred yards. There was a loud crash as the robot collided with the ground. Stormer glanced at the other security mechanoids and said, "Anyone else want to obstruct justice today?"

Furno leveled his plasma weapon. "Seriously, guys, no one needs to get hurt here. You can check with our headquarters, but we need to leave. I'll personally let your bosses know what a good job you did, okay?"

The security robots seemed to be thinking it over. In fact, they were receiving information from their home base. Their optic sensors had scanned Stormer and Furno in the first few seconds, transmitted their images and specifications, and were now receiving a response.

"Identities confirmed," said one of the robots. "Formal complaint will be filed with Hero Factory regarding damage to unit 411. You may pass."

As they walked away, Furno said, "I thought I was supposed to be the hothead and you were supposed to be the peacemaker."

"Just for future reference, most peacemakers don't negotiate while aiming a plasma weapon at someone."

"Maybe they should." Furno chuckled. "Deals get done a lot faster that way."

Stormer patched into his comm system. "Nex, are you there?"

Nex and Evo were back at base, coordinating the operations of the teams. There was only a brief pause before Stormer could hear his teammate's voice through his helmet communicator. "Nex here. What's the report?"

"He's been here and gone," said Stormer. "I have to assume he has the piece."

"Bulk is reporting failure on his end," Nex replied. "That means two of three, boss."

"I can add," snapped Stormer. "Anything from Stringer and Surge yet?"

"Negative, sir. But that ship graveyard is a notorious dead spot for communications. They probably won't be able to signal us until they're clear of it."

Stormer made a strategic decision. "All right. Contact Bulk. Tell him that he and Breez will meet up with Furno and myself at the graveyard. We will approach on the same vector Stringer is using, but meet just outside so we do not lose comm signal. We will then proceed to join up with Stringer and Surge. Got that?"

"Yes, sir. Transmitting now."

"You and Evo are on standby. If Core Hunter surprises us — if he makes for somewhere other than the freighter — you two are going to have to intercept him."

"Understood."

"Stormer out."

The Alpha Team leader turned to Furno. "We

have one last chance to stop him. If we fail, and he puts the pieces together . . ."

Stormer's voice trailed off. He looked troubled by more than just the obvious. After a few moments, he said, "It's too easy, Furno."

"What do you mean?"

"I know how Zib thinks it works—rebuild the weapon and, bam, universal destruction. I just . . . I don't think it could be quite that simple. We need to know more."

They were in sight of the Hero craft now. Furno sent the signal that would unlock the hatch and power up the ship. "Like what?" he said to Stormer.

"Core Hunter stole those three pieces years ago—how did he know where they were, or that they were valuable?" Before Furno could answer, Stormer had contacted Hero Factory once more. "Nex, contact Rocka. Tell him I have a job for him."

"Hey, look!"

Furno was pointing at the ship. Standing in front of it was a tall figure in a tattered robe. The stranger appeared to be unarmed and he made no threatening move, but Furno readied his weapon and advanced.

"Who are you? What are you doing near our ship?"

The figure simply nodded. "Courage. You will need that. The Heroes are moving in the right direction, Furno, but they are walking — they need to run."

"What do you know about all this?" demanded Stormer. "I want answers."

"Some things cannot be answered easily, no matter who is doing the asking," the figure replied. "But I will leave you with two words: Speeda Demon."

With that, the stranger vanished. A sensor sweep revealed no sign of him.

"Sir, Rocka is awaiting orders," Nex radioed.

"Right," said Stormer. "Tell him he's going to jail."

7

Its official name was Asteroid J-54, but everyone called it "the Stone."

After the mass breakout at Hero Factory, the prison there was temporarily shut down so repairs could be made. In the meantime, recaptured prisoners were being sent here, to the jail that existed before Hero Factory came into being. It was grim and old and forbidding, and Rocka could think of any number of places he would rather be. Still, the young Hero knew it was his job to follow Stormer's orders.

He knew the mission. Speeda Demon evidently knew something about what Core Hunter had stolen, but Speeda was still on the loose. Splitface, who was still imprisoned here, had once worked with him in a short-lived criminal team, so he might know something about what went on years before. He had recently been recaptured and thrown in jail. It was Rocka's job to make him talk.

Splitface was waiting in the small gray cell that was used as a visitor's area at J-54. He was muttering to himself, which wasn't unusual given that he had two personalities and they were often arguing with each other.

Rocka walked into the cell and slammed the iron door behind him. Splitface glanced up, contempt in his expression. Surge had captured him on the SIGMA SIGMA communications satellite, but it had been a tough fight. Splitface had been talking about escaping again ever since he'd landed at J-54.

"We need to talk," said Rocka.

"All right," Splitface answered, in a voice like gravel being ground to dust.

"Shut up!" Splitface said to himself, in a much

smoother voice. "It's me he wants to talk to, not you."

"Ha! Who would want to talk to you about anything?"

Rocka sighed. "I want to talk to whichever one of you knows Speeda Demon the best."

"That would be me," said the gravel voice. This time, there was no argument from his other personality.

"Did he ever know anything about a . . . treasure that was split up into three parts?" Rocka figured there was no point in telling Splitface he was asking about a weapon. "More importantly, did he tell someone else?"

"What's in this for us?" asked the smooth-voiced personality. "Why should we help you?"

"What do you want?"

"I want off J-54," said the gravel voice.

"Let me explain something to you," said Rocka, his voice quiet but his tone steel. "If you don't answer my question, by tomorrow there won't be a J-54, or an asteroid belt, or a Splitface, or anything else. Understand?"

"Yeah, I'm scared," said Splitface, sounding like he was anything but afraid. "But why not? What has Speeda Demon done for me? Sure, he bought some hunk of rock off a robot a long while back . . . supposed to be a map. Anyway, you know him, he hasn't the brains or the patience to figure out something like that. So he sold it to Core Hunter."

"What happened then?"

"Core Hunter acted like he knew what the whole thing was about. He mentioned some planet the map was supposed to be from, but I'd never heard of it before. When Speeda asked him what it was a map of, Core Hunter just laughed and told him he'd find out soon enough."

"And that was it?" Rocka asked. "Speeda Demon didn't try to find out what he had just sold?"

Splitface laughed. "He was already on to planning his next crime. His body moves fast, his mind moves faster, and neither one gets anywhere, know what I mean?"

That was all Splitface had to tell. With a little

more coaxing, and a promise of a bigger cell once he was back at Hero Factory, he revealed the name of the world Core Hunter had mentioned. That, Rocka decided, would be his next stop.

The planet Splitface had directed Rocka to was about as unpleasant a place as he could imagine. Great geysers of flame erupted from a surface studded with craters and ruined buildings. It looked like there had been a terrible war or natural disaster here some time back. There were no signs of any robot life anywhere.

Rocka had been hoping that someone on the world would be able to give him a hint of where to go next. Maybe there might have been a local legend about the map. With the whole place deserted, it was looking like this trip was a waste of time, and time wasn't something Alpha Team had a lot of right now.

One of his Hero craft sensors suddenly flared to life. There was a contact down below, a definite robot reading. If the instruments were to be believed, someone was on the surface who hadn't been there a moment before.

Rocka landed the Hero craft some distance away from the signal, bringing it in low in hopes that it wouldn't be spotted. Just as he landed, the sensor ping vanished, only to reappear right next to the ship. When Rocka emerged, a robed robot was waiting for him.

"Hero Factory," announced Rocka. "Who are you and what's your business here?"

"This is my world," said the stranger. "I think I should be asking you that."

"Are you alone here?"

"When I choose to visit, yes . . . unless others come with me."

"What happened here?" asked Rocka.

"I guess you could say I happened" was the reply. "It seems a craftsman can afford to make one error, but not two. The second left this planet uninhabitable, but the first . . . ah, that could do the same to the entire galaxy."

"You know about what Core Hunter is

seeking," said Rocka, taking aim with his cross-bow. "Are you in this with him?"

"I am helping you by helping him," the robot answered.

"Where is he?"

"Where he is doesn't matter, Rocka," said the robed figure. "All that matters is where he will be."

8

tringer and Surge charged down the corridors of the abandoned freighter. It had been a surprise when Stormer assigned Stringer to come back here. But the Alpha Team leader had explained that there was a chance the creature might have returned to the ship to nest at some point, and it would remember Stringer. That made him the obvious choice to go.

Of course, this time he wasn't alone. In addition to Surge, he had recruited a team of security robots from the company that managed the ship graveyard. This time, Core Hunter wasn't going to get away.

A sensor scan of the ship turned up no signs of

robot life at all, but an audio sweep had picked up sounds of movement. If it wasn't just space rats, it meant that Core Hunter might have found a way to block Hero Factory sensors.

Well, if anyone could, it would be him or Von Nebula, thought Stringer. *They're both ex–Hero Factory. Sometimes I wonder about our quality control. . . .*

"Spread out," he ordered. "No one but us has the okay to be here, so figure anything that moves probably isn't on board to throw a party for you. Go."

The security robots took off into the maze of corridors. Surge hung back. "I'll stay with you."

"It's okay, Surge, take off," said Stringer.

Surge shook his head. "He almost wiped you out the last time you faced him, and you know what happened to Bulk and Breez. Core Hunter's too dangerous to fight one-on-one."

Stringer glanced at Surge. He knew the kid was brave — you had to be to take down someone like Splitface on your own. But this place would give even Stormer a case of nerves. So maybe

Surge meant what he was saying, or maybe he just wanted someone watching his back. Either way, Stringer decided he was okay with that.

"Then let's get him," Stringer said, smiling.

Before they got very far in their search, their helmet communicators picked up the sound of blaster fire. It was coming from the starboard side of the ship. Stringer and Surge took off in a rush, only to run into an ambush of their own. Both Heroes ducked into doorways and fought back, Surge with electricity and Stringer with sonics.

"Who are those 'bots?" Surge asked, as laser fire just missed his head.

"Mercenaries," answered Stringer. "We recruited help and so did Core Hunter."

He spared a glance for his sensor pack. There was still no sign of the attackers, but the pinpoints of light that represented the security team were going out one by one. He had to assume they were outnumbered and outgunned at this point.

"Get back to the ship!" Stringer said. "Get it

out of the graveyard and call for help. I'll keep them off your back as long as I can."

"No way!" Surge answered. "I'm not leaving you behind!"

"Listen, kid, use your processor," Stringer said angrily. "If we both get junked, how is Hero Factory going to know he got the third piece? Somebody has to warn them so they can surround this ship and blow it up, if need be."

When Surge still didn't move, Stringer snapped, "I'm not asking you, kid — I'm telling you. Get out of here!"

"Stringer, I —"

"Go!"

Surge ran then, headed for the air lock and the Hero craft waiting on the other side. He tried to ignore the sounds of battle receding into the background as he moved and the idea that he might never see Stringer again. How would he face Stormer and the rest once they knew he had abandoned the veteran Hero to his fate?

He was just about to turn around and go back when two explosions knocked him off his feet.

When he had recovered, he saw the most amazing sight of his life: Stormer, Furno, Bulk, and Breez charging down the hallway toward him.

"Where's Stringer?" barked Stormer. "Report, rookie!"

Surge filled the team in on what he and Stringer had run into. Stormer nodded once, but said nothing as strategies took shape in his head.

"I didn't want to leave him," Surge finished. "He's pinned down."

"Not for long, he isn't," growled Bulk, already starting for the site of the battle.

"Back up Stringer, Bulk," Stormer ordered. "Furno, Surge, and I are going after Core Hunter. Breez, find Core Hunter's ship and disable it."

Bulk and Breez immediately took off in different directions.

"But how do we find him? Sensors aren't working," said Surge.

"I know where he is," said Stormer. "There's only one place he could be—the cargo hold where he and Stringer fought the creature. There would be a thousand places to hide the piece in there, plus it would suit his sense of humor to hide it right under Stringer's nose."

Furno called up a map of the ship on his scanner. "Based on Stringer's directions, it's on the other side of the ship. It will take us a long time—"

Stormer cut him off. "That's why you're going to melt us a path straight through to there, Furno. Maybe we can catch Core Hunter by surprise this time."

Furno fired up his plasma weapon and began burning through the metal walls of the ship. Steel melted like butter before his attack and the Heroes made rapid progress toward their destination. Once or twice, they stumbled upon some of Core Hunter's mercenaries, but electric bolts from Surge took the enemies out of the fight.

"Stormer, what if we're too late?" asked Surge.

"Then I'd suggest you hope there's some other galaxy to live in, because this one will be gone," answered the Alpha Team leader.

The rest of the journey was made in silence, save for the hiss of disintegrating metal. Each

Hero was alone with his thoughts. Furno was focused on the job at hand, but was also rehearsing for the battle to come. He would have to hit hard and fast and make sure Core Hunter got no chance to assemble the pieces. One misstep, one badly thought-out maneuver, and the fight would be lost.

For Stormer, it was all about betrayal. He had lived through Von Ness becoming Von Nebula, deserting Hero Factory, and then almost destroying it with his black-hole power. Now another ex-Hero, Core Hunter, was about to do much worse. Was the problem with their programming, he wondered, or was there something fundamentally wrong with Hero Factory? Were they asking too much of their team members, to the point where some of them just snapped and went bad? It wasn't something he could answer.

Surge's thoughts went down an even darker path. He had long worried that someday he might be tempted to become a villain. That was why he fought so hard against the villains who had escaped prison and why he was determined to be the one to take Core Hunter down. He had to prove—to Stormer, the others, and most importantly, himself—that he was a true Hero to the core.

"We're just about to break through," said Furno. "Get ready!"

"Nobody attacks without my say-so, got that?" said Stormer.

"Sure," said Furno.

"Yes, sir," said Surge.

The last wall dissolved into molten metal. Behind it was the vast open space of the cargo hold. In the center stood Core Hunter, hovering over an upended crate atop which two of the three pieces of the box were already assembled. He was holding the third piece, but making no move to add it on. Surrounding him were four armed robots, the type programmed to detect movement. As soon as the wall came down, they started firing their energy launchers.

"Take them—" yelled Stormer.

"Got 'em," shouted Surge, while firing his electricity shooter at the metal floor. The voltage traveled across the surface, shocking the opponents—all but Core Hunter, who leapt on top of a wooden crate with his recovered loot.

"Nice," the villain called out. "Then again, there are more where those came from— probably on their way here now, too."

A portion of the wall on the opposite side of the room suddenly caved in, thanks to a blow from Bulk. He and Stringer entered, weapons at the ready.

"Guess again," said Bulk. "We took care of all your little playmates on the way here. It's just you and us."

"Don't forget me," said Breez, standing in the doorway. She tossed a piece of metal onto the floor near Core Hunter. It was the fuel processor from his ship's engine, now a twisted wreck. "Sorry I'm late. I was doing some repair work on your vessel. Turns out I'm better at breaking things than fixing them."

Core Hunter chuckled softly. "So that's how it is, then? The gang's all here. You couldn't stand to miss my moment of triumph."

"We're here to shut you down," said Stormer.

"Resist arrest," said Furno. "Please. I've been looking forward to taking you out all day."

"I don't have to resist arrest, because all of you are going to walk away," said Core Hunter, lifting the partially completed box. "Or else I am going to put the third piece in place and . . ."

"No, you're not," said Stormer, with a confidence he didn't feel. "You want to live just as much as the rest of us."

"What makes you think I'll perish? It's mine now. It will do what I tell it to do."

Stormer started walking toward where Core Hunter perched. The other Heroes moved in as well. "You're crazy, or you're a fool," said Stormer. "Either way, that's too dangerous a toy for you to play with."

"Get back!" Core Hunter shouted, bringing the third piece to the point where it was almost touching the others. "Or the top ranks of Hero Factory will just be memories."

He's going to do it, Surge said to himself. *He's going to put that box together and it's going to do*

whatever it does, and that will be the end of every-
thing. I can't let him!

Before anyone could react, Surge unleashed a high-voltage shock blast at Core Hunter. At the last moment, the villain moved just enough to avoid taking the full charge. But what he got was enough to make his robot body spasm, and jam the third piece into the box, completing it.

"No . . ." whispered Core Hunter, as he realized what he had done.

"Blast that box!" shouted Stormer.

Six Hero Factory weapons were aimed and ready to fire. It was Bulk who stopped them, by saying, "Wait a minute . . . if that thing is back together, shouldn't something be happening?"

"Yes, it should," said Core Hunter, looking at the assembled box with contempt. "I think I've been ripped off."

"What a shame," said Stormer, smiling. "We'll just have to remove 'destroyed the galaxy' from your list of crimes, then."

The air beside Core Hunter began to shimmer. In the next instant, the robed figure appeared. Ignoring the Heroes, he spoke directly to the villain. "The box is not flawed . . . you have simply attempted to assemble it in the wrong place," he said.

"What are you talking about?" asked Core Hunter.

The figure took the box from him and broke it into pieces again. "It can only be assembled in the place in which it was made. Anywhere else, it will not function. I can send you where you need to go, Core Hunter, but you must assemble the box!"

"Hey, get that guy!" said Bulk.

The Heroes used their weapons to try to take down the new arrival. But the robed robot waved his hand and a force field appeared in midair, reflecting the Heroes' shots.

Meanwhile, Core Hunter was considering the offer. He didn't really want to put the box together — everything he had learned about it said that it was a weapon of devastating power. He just wanted to threaten to put it together, unless he was given vast amounts of money and rule of the known galaxy, among other things.

Now, though, all the Heroes knew he couldn't assemble the box unless he went where the robed robot told him to go. If he didn't accept the offer, he would have nothing to threaten them with. If he did accept it, his new helper would expect him to trigger the weapon.

In the end, it was a simple math problem. He could take care of one robot, weird powers or not, and then go ahead with his blackmail scheme a lot easier than fighting six Heroes on his own.

"Deal," he said.

"Stop them!" shouted Stormer, already racing toward the two. The other Heroes ran forward as well, but before they could get there, both Core Hunter and the box had winked out of existence.

Breez launched herself into the air and tackled the robed robot. "You're not going anywhere, friend. You're under arrest for aiding a fugitive, obstruction of justice, possession of a dangerous weapon, and anything else we can think of."

Her captive held up both his hands in

surrender. "There is no need for force. I will not fight you."

"Stormer, I know this guy," said Breez. "Bulk and I were just about to capture Core Hunter and this rat saved him."

"All right," said Stormer. "You're going to tell us where Core Hunter went and you're going to tell us now."

The robot got to his feet, under the watchful eyes of all six Heroes. "I will do better than that, Preston Stormer. I will take you there. But we must hurry, before he assembles the box. I sent him on a delayed teleport, yet I cannot be certain we will arrive in time."

"Wait a minute," said Furno. "Two seconds ago, you're giving Core Hunter tips on how to win, and now you're acting like you want to help us. What's the story?"

"I did what I had to do," was the reply. "If the box is assembled, it will turn intangible and begin to grow. Anything that lies in its path will find itself inside the box as it expands. When it reaches the limit of its expansion, it will turn solid and contract, crushing anything within."

"And what's the limit of its expansion?" asked Stringer. "How big can this thing get?"

"Once activated, it will not stop growing until it encompasses the entire galaxy. And then it will smash every star, every planet, and every living being to dust."

9

Stormer rapidly punched coordinates into the nav computer of the Hero craft. Behind him, the hooded figure silently watched.

"How do you know we can trust this guy?" asked Furno.

"I don't," said Stormer. "I'm guessing."

"You're betting the existence of the galaxy on a guess?!" exclaimed Bulk.

"If we throw him in jail, we're starting from scratch trying to find Core Hunter," Stormer answered, his eyes never leaving the ship's controls. "Do you like those odds? I don't. Besides, I think I have figured part of this out. Core Hunter tried to put the box together, but it didn't work. Why not? Because something was missing—it had to be."

Stormer glanced at the hooded figure. He wasn't nodding, but he wasn't shaking his head either, so Stormer went on.

"My guess is something got released when the box was split into three pieces—some sort of energy—and the box needs to draw that back in, in order to function. That's why he has to go back to where the thing was first created."

"And tall, dark, and scary here told him where it was," said Breez. "How helpful."

The hooded figure turned to her. Then he slowly reached up and removed the hood. Beneath it was a robotic face of a design none of them had seen before, indescribably ancient yet somehow still radiating sheer power. "It was the only way," said the figure. "My name is Arctur. I built the doom box . . . and now you must destroy it."

The questions rained down thick and fast on Arctur as Stormer pushed the ship for every bit of speed he could get. It was Bulk who demanded to know why, given how dangerous the device was, anyone would tell a known villain where to go to reassemble it.

"Think of who he is and what he does," said Arctur. "He draws out Hero Cores and somehow contains their energies. That means he may be able to contain the energy of the box as well. But there was no way to convince him to help save the galaxy, so I pretended to aid him in its conquest."

"And stopped us from stopping him," Bulk shot back.

"I did what was necessary," Arctur replied.

"If you hadn't built the thing in the first place—"

"Enough!" snapped Stormer. "We're here."

The assembled Heroes looked down at the fiery wreck of a planet. Then, as one, they looked at Arctur.

"You did this?" asked Breez. "How do you live with yourself?"

"Sometimes, you have no choice but to go on, Breez, if only to try to atone," Arctur replied. "I have been chasing the doom box for more years than Hero Factory has been in existence. Perhaps today the chase will come to an end."

With some effort, Stormer brought them in for a landing in one of the few clear spots on the surface. Arctur pointed them toward the underground complex where the box had been created five millennia ago. Furno did a quick scan.

"This place is a maze," he reported. "Core Hunter is still hiding from our sensors. How are we supposed to find him?"

"I can guide you," said Arctur. "I know where he has to be going."

Stormer nodded to the others, indicating it was all right to follow their new ally. He really didn't see any other choice. The chances of tracking down Core Hunter on their own were next to none.

The team moved as quickly as they could through the almost pitch-dark tunnels. As they traveled, Bulk moved up next to Arctur and whispered, "So why would you build something like this in the first place? I can't really see any use for it besides destroying things."

Arctur glanced down at the floor, looking almost ashamed. "My friends and I believed we were better suited to rule this world than those in power. The box was intended as a way of eliminating those who stood in our way. Put in the proper places and activated remotely, it would effectively make anyone or anything we didn't like disappear.

"But there was a flaw in its construction. It couldn't be shut off. Used even once, it would leave nothing of our galaxy. That is why we tried to destroy it."

"I have a sensor reading up ahead, closing fast," said Furno. "Maybe Core Hunter has another little helper."

"No," said Stormer. "Actually, I think we do."

Rocka suddenly appeared out of the darkness. "Am I glad to see you! Core Hunter showed up a couple of minutes ago. He's got all three pieces, but he hasn't put them together yet."

"He must!" said Arctur. "Only by activating the box can the energies be siphoned and the device rendered harmless."

"And how do you suggest we encourage him to destroy the galaxy?" asked Stringer.

"Maybe . . ." Surge began, then stopped.

Stormer glanced at the rookie. He had come down on him pretty hard on the way here about his error on the freighter. It was a stupid mistake that could have had terrible consequences. He could see in Surge's eyes that the Hero's confidence was damaged.

"Go ahead, Surge," said Stormer. "Maybe what?"

"Maybe . . . we don't give him any choice," answered Surge. "You know him better than anyone—you, Bulk, and Stringer. What if the alternative was bad enough that destroying everything seemed like a better choice?"

A small smile came to Bulk. "You know, Stormer, maybe the kid's got something. We push his buttons hard enough—"

"He'll snap," Stringer finished for him. "He likes being the big, bad bounty hunter everyone's afraid of . . . what if we could take that away from him?"

"Whatever we're going to do, let's do it now," said Rocka. "I don't like leaving him alone with that thing."

"Arctur, you stay out of this," said Stormer. "This is a Hero Factory matter now."

"And you do not trust me, my friend?" Arctur answered, smiling. "Well, I would think less of you if you felt any other way."

Following Rocka's lead, the seven Heroes raced for the central chamber. There was Core Hunter, pieces in hand, studying them like an archaeologist might ponder a rare find.

"You know, it's really quite beautiful, in a terrible sort of way," he said. "Three pieces of insignificant rubbish, which when joined together make the ultimate weapon. It sort of reminds me of Hero Factory in the old days, Stormer—all of us were just a collection of parts on our own, but together . . . oh, was there anything we couldn't do together?"

"Keep you from going bad," replied Stormer.

"Is that regret I hear, team leader?" Core Hunter chuckled.

"No," said Stringer. "Just pity."

"Watch it," warned Core Hunter.

Furno took a step forward. "What for? We all know you don't have the core to put that box together. You're just a thief and a launcher-for-hire. Galactic destruction is out of your league."

Core Hunter's eyes narrowed. "Tell him, Stormer. Tell him about the number of Heroes whose cores I've taken over the years. I'm someone to be respected, feared even . . . *never* pitied."

Stormer steeled himself. It was time to play his big bluff. "Is that what you think? You're a bigger fool than I thought."

"What are you babbling about?" demanded Core Hunter.

"We used you," said Stormer, emphasizing each word. "Any Hero who couldn't beat you just wasn't good enough for Hero Factory. We let you weed out the losers for us."

"You're . . . you're lying," said Core Hunter. "I've been on your 'Most Wanted' list for years."

Bulk laughed. "Hey, we had to make it look good, didn't we? All those stiffs whose cores you took—we patched 'em up and now they're working as guard robots or maintenance mechs. So I guess we should say thanks—after all, they might have folded fighting someone really tough and we would have had to clean up the mess."

Core Hunter looked from one Hero to another, looking for some sign that he was being tricked. All he saw were stone-faced stares. It was ridiculous—it was impossible—but it was also just the sort of thing he imagined Hero Factory would do.

"Of course, after all this, well, you've gotten out of control," said Stormer. "You actually think you're some kind of master criminal, instead of the small-timer you've always been. So this time, when we put you away, you won't be getting out. And we'll have to make sure everyone knows that you've been . . . working for us all this time."

Stormer's words hit Core Hunter like a physical blow. His reputation, all he had worked for all these years, would be in tatters. He would be laughed at by every other criminal, and that was if he was lucky. They might think he had been informing for Hero Factory, too, and decide to take him apart.

"No, no," he said, desperation creeping into his voice. "I don't believe you. Prove it."

"We don't have to," said Stringer. "All we have to do is convince enough other folks that it's true."

"Maybe we should put him on Hero Factory spacecast," suggested Furno. "You know, make sure everyone knows what he looks like, just in case we get bored and let him escape again."

"Let me . . . ?" said Core Hunter. "That's enough! Before you can wreck everything I am, everything I stand for, I'll see all of you on the junk pile — starting with you, Stormer!"

Core Hunter fired an energy blast at the Alpha Team leader. Just as it was about to strike him, Arctur leapt in its path, taking the blow himself. He collapsed on the ground, smoke coming from his chestplate. Breez rushed over to him.

"He's in bad shape," she said to Stormer. "We need to get him to a repair station off-planet."

"No time . . ." Arctur said weakly. "But maybe

I finally . . . made up for all I've done . . . at least a little."

Core Hunter laughed. "That's just the start, Heroes. You wanted to ruin me? I will ruin everything."

The villain snapped the three pieces of the box together. Instantly, it began to glow. Core Hunter let it go and the box floated in midair. Then it slowly began to expand, and Core Hunter found his right hand disappearing inside of it.

"Quickly," whispered Arctur. "His weapon . . . Core Hunter's weapon . . . use it now!"

"Breez, go!" said Stormer.

Launching herself into the air, Breez flew to where Core Hunter stood, with at least half his body having been absorbed into the box. She grabbed his left hand, which still held the device he used to remove Hero Cores. Forcing his hand to the trigger, she activated the weapon.

The core remover hummed to life. To the astonishment of the assembled Heroes, a green mist began to coalesce around the end of the weapon. As Arctur had predicted, Core Hunter's weapon was drawing to it the energies of the doom box.

"Is it working?" asked Furno anxiously.

"I don't . . ." Rocka began. "No, wait— I think the box is shrinking!"

It was indeed. Still immaterial, the box was reducing in size and releasing its hold on Core Hunter as its energy poured into his weapon. The villain was struggling to free himself from Breez's grip, but she hung on as the rest of the Heroes closed in.

Finally, the box was back to its original size. It dropped to the ground, splitting back into three pieces again. Its threat at last was over.

The danger was not.

"Um, is Core Hunter's weapon supposed to be doing that?" asked Rocka.

The villain's core remover was glowing green now, supercharged with the energy of the box. Core Hunter was looking at it with a mixture of wonder and fear.

"The power," he muttered. "So much power... enough to tear a galaxy apart."

"Oh boy," said Stringer. "Times like this, I wonder why it is I love this job."

Core Hunter flung Breez off his back and swept the other Heroes away with a wave of his weapon. His optic sensors blazed with madness.

"You were right, Stormer," he said, raising his weapon. "I was small-time—but I'm not anymore!"

"Down!" yelled Stormer. The Heroes hit the ground just as an emerald green bolt of energy flew from Core Hunter's weapon. It struck a wall of the chamber, disintegrating it, then flew on, blasting the next wall it encountered and the next and the next.

"Blazes," exclaimed Furno. "According to my sensors, it wiped out two solid miles of this complex before burning out!"

"Cores, cores," laughed Core Hunter. "Trivial little things, just as you all are. Now I can hunt bigger things—stars, worlds, entire solar systems. And I have Hero Factory to thank for it. To show my gratitude, I won't force you to live through my reign—I will end your existences now."

With that, the villain unleashed blast after blast of his newfound energy, blasting holes in the floor, the ceiling, and the other walls. He wasn't even trying to hit the Heroes, just unleashing destruction for the sake of destruction. Worse, the effort did not seem to lessen his power at all.

"Let's go, Heroes," yelled Stormer. "They can't all be easy ones. Take him!"

Stringer and Bulk charged. Core Hunter caught Bulk with a glancing blow from his energy beam, sending the powerful Hero flying a quarter mile through ruined walls. Stringer unleashed a sonic assault, only to have the villain blast the floor underneath him, sending him tumbling down into the bowels of the complex.

Now it was Furno and Breez's turn. Furno fired his plasma weapon, hoping to melt Core Hunter's core remover, while Breez distracted the foe with an aerial attack. Core Hunter used his energies to knock Breez out of the air, right into the path of one of Furno's blasts. She cried out and lay still. In anguish, Furno raced to her side, only to have the villain bring the ceiling down on top of both of them.

Stormer, Surge, and Rocka moved to the attack from three sides. But Core Hunter was ready for them. "I used to have to remove your Hero Cores to take your energy," said the villain. "But now I can steal your energy over distance . . . or have you already found that out?"

Rocka and Stormer were finding it hard to move, as if their legs weighed tons. Their internal power monitors were falling at an alarming rate. Powerless, both Heroes dropped like stones.

Within a matter of seconds, everyone was down but Surge. He stood facing Core Hunter, knowing he was completely overpowered. The right move would be to flee for the Hero craft and signal Zib to send reinforcements. But Surge wasn't going to run, not this time, even if it would've been the smartest course of action. He would stand or fall with his team.

"I know about you," Core Hunter said slowly. "You're the one who attacked me on the freighter.

I'll bet Stormer chewed you out about that, didn't he?"

Surge said nothing.

"I've been there. I know how it feels to be unappreciated by your commander. Why do you think I left Hero Factory? There was nothing for me there and no one who cared about my future."

Core Hunter took a step toward Surge. "Well, I care about your future, Surge. Trust me, anywhere else but at my side, you don't have one. Leave them to their well-deserved fate and be the first of my new army. You can be a general, leading my troops to the conquest of Makuhero City."

Here it was, the moment Surge had been dreading for all of his short career. He was standing on the border of darkness and light. Opposing Core Hunter meant certain destruction, but siding with him would mean abandoning everything he had ever said he stood for. It would be simple to give in — that was the power of evil: It always made everything look easy.

I could do it, thought Surge. *Part of me might*

even want to—but if I do, what then? My friends will be destroyed as surely as if I had doomed them. When I look in a mirror, I won't see Mark Surge, Hero, anymore. I won't see anything. I'll just be an empty metal shell, no better than Splitface or Speeda Demon . . . or Core Hunter.

"No," Surge answered at last. "Hero Factory isn't perfect. Neither am I. But we're not so imperfect that I would turn to someone like you. Oh, and one more thing—you're under arrest."

Core Hunter smiled. Then he laughed, for a long time. Without warning, his laughter was cut off and he was aiming and firing his weapon at Surge.

The Hero responded the only way he could, unleashing a blast of high-voltage electricity. Power met power and, incredibly, Core Hunter actually staggered a bit. Surge thought maybe he just might win, until he saw his foe was still smiling.

"More energy," said Core Hunter. "With a little oil, it would make a meal."

Then the expression on Core Hunter's face

slowly changed. At first, it was dismay; then fear; then agony creased his robotic features. Something was very wrong, and suddenly his triumph was slipping through his metal fingers like sand.

"What . . . what did you do . . . you fool?" he choked.

"I don't know," Surge admitted.

"The power is feeding back . . . too much power to contain . . . pouring into me . . . help me . . ."

Surge rushed to his side, but found he couldn't get too close because of the fearsome emerald energies now radiating from Core Hunter. Stormer or Stringer might know what to do in this situation, but both were unconscious thanks to the villain.

"I can't help you," said Surge. "You defeated the only ones who could. There's . . . nothing anyone can do now."

"Wanted to conquer . . . to rule . . . not just fade away," Core Hunter said, his voice growing fainter by the second.

Before Surge could answer, the energies flared so brightly that his optic sensors were almost overloaded. When he could see again, it was to behold a frightening and incredible sight — Core Hunter seemed to actually fold in on himself, again and again, growing smaller and smaller until he was just a pinpoint in space. Then even that — and the energies that caused it — had disappeared.

Surge stood staring at the empty spot in the air for a long, long time.

Epilogue

mission Log, Stormer recording. Although there is no reason to believe it has not been disarmed, we have transported the doom box back to Hero Factory for safekeeping.

Despite Zib's best efforts, we have been unable to discover the fate of Core Hunter. He may have been destroyed, converted into some other form of matter, or transported to another dimension.

Sole casualty of this operation was the being designated Arctur. My team has largely recovered from their injuries. I am recommending Surge for a commendation. Despite his earlier error, he faced his personal demons on this mission and overcame *them. No more can be asked of any Hero.*

Stormer clicked off the recorder. On his monitor screen was a picture of Core Hunter from his days as a Hero. He looked happy. Stormer wondered if he ever really was, before or after leaving Hero Factory.

"What makes someone like that go bad?"

Stormer turned to see Surge standing in the doorway. The rookie looked troubled.

"If I knew, it wouldn't happen again," he replied. "Maybe they want too much from being a Hero . . . or not enough. Maybe they just can't follow someone else's rules—*anyone* else's rules. Or could be some flaw in the design, something so small we can't find it anywhere in Assembly Tower."

"Did you . . . you know . . . ever think about it?"

Stormer turned back to the screen. "Honestly? No. This was the work I was born to do. It's what makes me more than a collection of parts. It's what gives me a soul . . . and you, too."

For the first time since their return to Hero

Factory, Surge managed a smile. "Yeah, and me, too. It's funny — even though he was super-powerful in that fight, maybe I could somehow sense it was going to end. That's how it ends for all of them — in jail, or dismantled, or on the run for the rest of their lives. That's not the existence I want for myself."

Now it was Stormer's turn to smile. "You have a lot more, and a lot better, waiting for you than that, Surge. Your teammates believe in you. So do I."

Surge started to say thank you, but Stormer cut him off.

"Hey," said the Alpha Team leader. "Just because things worked out doesn't mean you didn't screw up. You're on double training sessions with Bulk all week, got it?"

"Yes, sir, and —"

"Dismissed."

Stormer waited until he heard Surge's footsteps receding in the hallway. Then he punched a button on his console and watched the image of Core Hunter slowly fade away on his screen.

"So long, Hero," he said. "If not happiness, I hope you've at least found peace. That's something that's in short supply in this galaxy."

Stormer hit another button. The images of escaped criminals still at large appeared on the monitor. After studying them for a moment, he pressed the comm button.

"Stringer, this is Stormer. Assemble the team. We still have work to do."

The adventure continues in

SECRET MISSION #2:
LEGION OF DARKNESS

When Hero Factory starts making things hard for villains, Black Phantom realizes that the criminals need a team of their own. From every corner of the galaxy, he assembles an army of criminals. Their mission: wipe Hero Factory right off the map. Outnumbered and out-powered, the Heroes Thresher, Von Ness, Stringer, Bulk, and Stormer must come up with a way to win—or else see the galaxy become an empire of crime.

Bulk walked into the meeting room, pausing in the doorway to look around. It was a stark, bare room with bright white lighting overhead. One other robot was already there, a tall one with gray armor. Bulk sat down next to him and extended a hand.

"Hi, my name's Bulk," said the broad-shouldered robot. "Three guesses why."

The gray-armored robot smiled as he shook his hand. "Von Ness. Any idea what this is all about?"

Bulk shook his head. "I just got out of the Assembly Tower an hour ago. But considering all the weapons they gave us, I doubt we're going to be tending flower beds."

Von Ness chuckled. "Not unless the weeds around here have rocket launchers."

Another robot, this one with black armor, came in. He sat a few seats away from Bulk and Von Ness. He was followed shortly by Stormer, who nodded to all three and busied himself setting up a holographic presentation.

When this was done, he sat down in the front row.

Thresher came in a few minutes later. He gave a brief smile to the assembled robots and stood at the front of the room to address them. "For those of you who don't know me, my name is Thresher. Going around the room, we have Stormer, Stringer, Bulk, and Von Ness here. Welcome, all of you, to Hero Factory."

Bulk and Von Ness gave each other quizzical looks. Stringer shifted in his chair, looking a little bored.

"All of you are to be members of Alpha Team, the first active Hero Factory squad," Thresher continued. "It will be our job to keep the galaxy safe from thieves, smugglers, and worse. Criminals can be found all over, on every world. If you're expecting glory, the door is over there — this is not about personal glory. If you're expecting to become a legend, same answer — the odds are, none of us will be remembered past the day we are decommissioned."

Thresher looked at each of the new Heroes in turn. "But if you want to feel like you made a difference, this is the place for you. If you want to power down at night knowing that traders, travelers, and working robots are a little bit safer because of something you did, then you are the kind of Hero I need on my squad." He paused for a moment, then said, "Any questions?"

Stringer raised his hand. "Just one, Chief—who asked for us?"

"I don't understand, Stringer," Thresher said.

Stringer stood up. "See, I've been scanning datafiles on a lot of the worlds out there while I was waiting for this meeting. Quite a few of these planets we're supposed to be protecting are getting rich by hiding criminals, or giving them a place to stash their loot, or selling them ships and arms when they need them. They sure aren't going to want us around. So who is it that's calling for a factory that makes Heroes?"

"Can I answer that?" Stormer asked Thresher.

"Go ahead."

Stormer got to his feet and turned to Stringer. "I understand what you're saying, but you're looking at things the wrong way. Those planets you talked about — they are working with criminals because they see no other choice. The law can't protect them. The average robot can't stand up to someone like Splitface or Voltix and hope to survive intact. So they play along. These aren't the places that will turn us away. They are the places that need us the most!"

Bulk looked over his shoulder. He expected Stringer to continue the argument or make some smart remark. Whoever this Stormer was, he sure took the whole Hero thing seriously. But instead, Stringer was just smiling, not in a nasty way, but more like he admired the guts Stormer had shown in giving that answer. In that moment, Bulk decided that Stringer was okay.

Von Ness raised his hand. "What are the odds, Thresher? I don't mind fighting. I do mind losing."

Thresher activated the holographic projector. It displayed a miniature map of the galaxy, studded with points of red light. There seemed to be hundreds of thousands of them. "Each light you see indicates that a crime was committed in that spot sometime in the last year. So to answer your question, the odds of success are pretty low. Until Hero Factory is running full force and we have more help, it's going to be the five of us against an awful lot of bad guys."

"And we think we have a chance because . . . ?" asked Von Ness.

"We're a team," said Stormer. "They're not. The plan is simple: Hero Factory will take them on one by one and beat them all."

"That's a plan?" said Von Ness, disbelief in his voice.

"And a good one," Stormer answered, with a smile.